In Search of
Biddy Early

EDMUND LENIHAN

THE MERCIER PRESS
CORK and DUBLIN

The Mercier Press Limited
4 Bridge Street, Cork
24 Lower Abbey Street, Dublin 1

© Edmund Lenihan, 1987

British Library Cataloguing in Publication Data
Lenihan, Edmund
  In search of Biddy Early
  1. Early, Biddy (Legendary character)
  2. Tales—Ireland
  I. Title
  398'.352   GR153.5

  ISBN 0-85342-820 4

Printed by Litho Press Co., Midleton, Co. Cork.

Contents

Introduction

There are still people today who would not for the life of them step over a child playing on the kitchen floor, because it might stunt the child's growth. Others leave a morsel of food at the side of their plates 'for the Holy Souls'. Yet others feel that they are being talked about if their noses itch, and even the most hardened cynics will acknowledge a black cat rather than a tabby or make a quick decision as to whether to pass under a ladder even though no one is working on it.

Then there are the churchgoers, sincere people who, though they pray to a God unseen, unheard, would take offence at any deep and firmly-held belief in the Good People or otherworldly manifestations not of a formally religious kind. Few of them would agree that by denying belief in the latter they might be calling into question their own most closely-held beliefs. Some would say that if fairies *do* exist – 'And we by no means admit it' – they are the power of evil showing itself and should be shunned. However, a case such as the one I am about to examine, that of Biddy Early, shows quite clearly that Biddy did good for all and sundry. An old man from near Kilkishen stated the case succinctly for me:

"'Twas good things she done all the time. Sure, the Devil never cured anyone, only made 'em worse if he could. He has nothing to give you only what he has himself. That's his trade.'[1]

This is an opinion I heard echoed again and again on my travels. In all the stories related to her which I have collected, only one could be said to prove that she used her power irresponsibly (see p. 57) and even in this one case there are mitigating circumstances.

However, whether her power was of Good or Evil, few would dispute the claim that she had some gift out of the ordinary and that she used it frequently. Those who can believe that nineteenth century rural Ireland was populated by a benighted peasantry ruled over by tyrannical priests and hemmed in by taboos and fears of dark and scarcely-understood powers will find no difficulty in believing that Biddy herself was also a victim of these same constraints and shadows. Perhaps she was, but the image that comes down the decades is of a woman who saw further than her contemporaries, both the ignorant and those who considered themselves educated.

Enigmatic, she slips in and out of our view, and even when we get a sustained look at her during her years in Kilbarron we are still confined to viewing the surface of what must have been a complex personality. But conclusions *can* be drawn, based on the accounts that remain among the grandchildren, occasionally the children, of those who knew her. It is because I have faith in these accounts that I have relied exclusively on the spoken word and thereby dispensed with a bibliography. The decision was a conscious one, and for two reasons: (1) because the concensus of opinion among so many people living far apart carried, to me, a certain kind of conviction, and (2) because I felt this to be a timely occasion to collect and present such opinions since the last of that generation is now passing away who could say with certainty that their grandparents, or even parents, knew Biddy or visited her. Such a collection may be of service to whoever undertakes to say the last word on the matter – should such a task ever be attempted!

My own opinion as to the truth or otherwise of the stories which I have collected is, briefly: in many cases, what Biddy is purported to have done is what an oppressed peasantry would themselves wish to have done if they had dared, for example, standing up to the police or the landlord or putting the priest in his place. (It is no accident, I think, that today the best known of all the stories associated with Biddy is the one in which she sticks the priest and his horse to the road.) In short, around Biddy gathered the group-fantasies and wishes of her own people, and once her fame had started to spread, other stories of a more general sort also attached themselves to her, e.g. the story of the pig (p. 45-46) and that of the power-contest (p.104). These are to be found in many parts of Ireland where Biddy is only a name. Lady Gregory, I think, was correct when almost seventy years ago, she foretold that the fame of Biddy would grow as time went on and that some of the myths that hang always in the air would gather round her. I hope that this collection proves the accuracy of both her prophecies and also goes some way towards reminding a present-day audience that Biddy was a real person of flesh and blood, since there is a danger that with her passing into the lore of general currency she may become a semi-mythological figure.

She was a person (albeit an extraordinary one) who lived a reasonably normal life among reasonably normal people, yet the question remains: was she 'in the fairies' or merely a messenger used by them? Some of the stories have her using the familiar 'we' when speaking of them, but this is not in itself conclusive since many others show her holding her distance from them. More to the point is the growing belief, forced on me by the writing of this book, that even in a technological age such as ours much survives of belief in a different way of looking at life. It is a view that sees events as having a logic that is not scientific or mathematical, that sees a world undetected by the strongest microscope; a world , in short, that is parallel to ours, but no whit less real for being invisible to us, a world that crosses ours only in certain times and places and through the inter-mediacy of certain people – such as Biddy Early. We occasionally get glimpses of what the inhabitants of this world may be like, for example there must be gradations and degrees of importance since Biddy could not thwart the power of some such as the Fool of the Fairies (see p. 38) or the Coolmeen Lake Witch (see p. 39). There is also an indication that the Good People gave nothing for nothing. The note of panic in Biddy's voice which conveys itself in the anecdote on p. 59 suggests that she was walking a tightrope between the demands of suppliants on her and how much she could safely ask of the Good People. They had feelings, as we see from p. 35, and they could be jealous, even malignant in defence of their power, as seen in their frequent treatment of Biddy:

'I often heard it said that she never gave out a cure but the Good People didn't give her a fierce gruelling after it.'[2]

All this, I hope, will become clear as the story unfolds.

There was no conscious decision on my part to write this book; rather the necessity for it became clearer to me over a period of eight years, the time I have spent collecting folklore in the Midwest region. From the first day I heard of Biddy Early but took no great notice. But gradually it began to dawn on me that here was a person who was known by literally everyone, if only by name. I soon began to seek out specific information on her and was even myself surprised at the quantity which built up over a very few years. However, I would probably have gone on happily collecting for another decade had not a few coinciding events brought my interest into sharper focus. The first of these occurred recently when I was collecting information for Part 3 of my *Parish Survey of Otherworldly Clare*. I was referred, in passing, to a woman who would, I was assured, be able to tell me much about Biddy. I duly visited her and she agreed to help, telling me to call back in a week's time. When I did so, her attitude had changed completely. She refused to talk to me. I persisted in asking why and was told that two days after I had spoken with her she had fallen and hurt herself. This she took as a friendly warning from Biddy to divulge nothing.

Then there was the man in the town of Ennis who conducted all his business with me from behind a locked door. Our encounter went as follows:

'I'm told you might be able to tell me a few stories.'

'What kind o' stories?'

'Stories about Biddy Early.'

'Biddy Early? You must be jokin'. F— off!'

And I did. End of interview. Yet I could not help but be struck by the oddness of these reactions. They whetted my appetite rather than discourage me. At about the same time, while visiting friends in Kilnamona near Ennis, a fairy fort called the *Liosachán* was pointed out to me on their land. It was said to be very 'airy', but had the added distinction of having been called 'the only real fort in Clare' by none other than Biddy herself. Why, nobody knows. Intriguing!

On another occasion, on my way to Athlone I stopped off at Ballylee to call at Yeats' tower, and there I happened to overhear an old woman claim that Biddy had said –

'There's a cure for every known evil between the two millstones of Ballylee.'

The woman knew no more than that. Again, intriguing.

But the final decider to go ahead was provided by a woman near Tulla. I stopped at her house quite at random to ask for directions and her first words on opening the door were 'You're looking for stories o' Biddy. She was a bad woman an' you'd be better off to stay away from her.'

I was speechless. This was exactly what Biddy herself had done to many a visitor to her own door over a century before, told out name and business before a word had been spoken by him. I confess that I did feel uneasy then, far more so than I was ever to feel later in the face of all the friendly warnings from well-meaning people to 'leave her alone'. It is not a comfortable thing to feel that your innermost motives can be seen so transparently. In the next ten minutes, as I heard Biddy blamed for the woman's present misfortune in being badly housed due to the advice of an old man many years ago who said that an original and better site should not be used because Biddy had rested there on one of her trips from Tulla to Ennis, I began to see that she was a presence which still touches people's lives. And not merely the credulous and superstitious, either. The very cats and dogs of Clare know that the reason why Clare hasn't won an All-Ireland senior hurling title since 1914 is because Biddy said they wouldn't until the last member of that team died. The fact that they did not win in all the years since was taken as proof of her power, only no one bothered to ask how a woman who had died in 1874 could have made such a prophecy in 1914 – forty years after her own death. Strange faith! Or is it a proof of something else, a blurring of the distinction between myth and fact? The growing realisation that this was indeed the case is what finally made me collect as many of the stories as I could. What we have today are fragments compared to the abundance that was available even a generation ago. With the passing of *cuaird* the memory is no longer refreshed or the repertoire added to by constant retelling.

The last of those who knew Biddy personally had passed away by the mid 1950s, but it might seem that there should still be enough people available whose recent ancestors went to Biddy for one reason or another. And this is certainly so. But the changes that have occurred in the past quarter-century have, by their rapidity, disrupted all orderly change, and those who might be expected to know the past in detail often do not. Frequently one meets them in surroundings that are not conducive to conversation let alone storytellng, environs where radio or television are too often used to drown out the silence of loneliness, in hospitals and rest-homes. Rarely can they be found now in groups of their own equals where the circle and store of knowledge is a mutual thing and 'one thing brings down another.' Now one has a sense of collecting the fragments of what was once vital, pieces that no longer make up a complete picture. One is fishing in the puddles of an all but dried-up channel, the river having long ago flowed in another direction. It is for this reason that I have not tried to write a biography of Biddy, and it will also, I hope, account for the fact that some periods of her life are scarcely mentioned while others are dealt with at length. Quite simply, I have matched my account to the oral material available to me and have not attempted to fill the gaps from written records. This would hardly be possible, in any case, since details about her life are very sparse, and it would not fit my purpose, which is to give an indication of what remains of Biddy in the folk-memory now.

My approach has always been that something can be saved from the ravages of time, and *must* be, since what is now available, though less than yesterday, is still more than tomorrow's remnants. In this spirit I present the following stories to the reader. It has been my aim throughout to remain in the background as much as possible, to let those who know speak for themselves. And they are remarkably well able to do so, most of them having a gift of dramatisation that was a vital part of the storytelling tradition. Note, for example, that not one of them reports what Biddy said. They all put words in her mouth, each one regarding these as her very utterance. The very stuff of drama!

In an effort to preserve as far as possible the actual speaking voice of the teller I have only minimally standardised spelling etc. That is the least I could do for those who took the trouble to make my search such an enjoyment and instruction.

E. Lenihan
Crusheen, Co. Clare
February 1987

1: Early Years

Biographical material on Biddy's early years is difficult to come by as part of the oral tradition nowadays. I think it may always have been relatively scarce in comparison with the many pieces of information available about her later life, but there is no mystery in this. In all probability Biddy was so indistinguishable from her young contemporaries that there was nothing of note to record. In any case it was not an age of pen and paper for people such as hers. Little survives of most ordinary people of the early twentieth century – a few official entries in parish registers and hardly anything more – so we must not expect too much of the early nineteenth century. And if she did, from an early age, show an affinity for the Good People and things otherworldly, well, that was no cause for undue worry in an age when belief in such was strong in adults, never mind children.

That she was born near the beginning of the new century seems not to be in doubt:

'She was born in 1798 in Faha, Biddy O'Connor.'[3] Also:

'She was Bid Connors. She was born above in Faha – that's a-near Kilanena. My mother knew her well. Why wouldn't she! They had only a small little haggart where she was born. They call it today Máire's haggart, in Faha. The oul' ruins o' the house is there still but 'tis only an oul' *cabhail* (shell).'[4]

However, though Faha is now generally regarded as her birthplace, there have been other claims. The following is one such:

''Tis tradition that the Earlys lived in a place called Carrowroe. Well now, that was a small townland between Gorteen an' Moymore, an' between Daingean an' Lisofinn. If you go up to Moymore cross an' turn to your left about five hundred yards from the cross there's two little fields there. Two acres that's in each o' the fields an' there's a wall between the two, a sort of a bushy, gappy wall. But, there was a field of it next the road an' there was a bit of a stone wall about four feet high an' about three or four yards long dividing the fields an' meeting the road wall at right angles. But, back a couple o' yards in the wall that's dividing the two fields there's a bit of a mortared wall, 'twould be no more than three feet

high. An' in the road wall there's another bit of mortared wall. That
was supposed to be where Biddy Early was born.'[5]

Nothing certain is known about her thereafter until she came to
Carheen – or Ayle – as a servant-girl. Who she worked for there is
the subject of some dispute, as the following accounts show:

'She went down from Faha, down to Feakle, oh, I suppose about
sixteen or seventeen years of age, working out, you know. They
were poor at home. An' she went down to Dr Dunne. He was the
Feakle doctor an' he lived in Kilbarron, in the big house that was
in it that time. I don't think that he owned all the estate that was
there, because there was 150 acres o' land in it. He could have the
house rented, you know, from some oul' gentleman. But he had a
few cows in it, an' calves, an' a pony an' trap.'[6]

'She lived up here above, about two miles from here, in Biddy
Early's haggart, above where Joyce has. She lived there. 'Tis in
Carheen, in Ayle, partly. She was there before she went to Kilbar-
ron.'[7]

Whether she went to Kilbarron immediately after leaving Ayle is
also disputed, as will be seen, but for the moment she had employ-
ment. Was she working now to help her parents at home in Faha,
or were they still alive at this time? No oral account survives to tell
us. The only hint we have that she was by now on her own occurs
in the following account, where we see her paying rent. If she were
a domestic servant the likelihood is that she would have been provided with accommodation. Another interesting feature of this
account is that it has Biddy possessing her famous bottle at this time.
More about that later. P. Minogue takes up the story:

'Now there was an oul' landlord, Sheehy, an' he was going to
evict all the people around Ayle. He used to come an' go from
Limerick in his pony an' trap an' he was coming late one evening
here to Ayle to stay for the night. But, he had to pass through the
Mills on his way, an' the Mills peelers told him "Ah, you shouldn't
go back to Ayle at all tonight." "Why?" "'Tisn't safe." "Well,
lookit," says he, "I'm more afraid o' the dogs of Ayle than I am o'
the people of Ayle." "D'you want protection, so?" "No." So the
next thing was, the tenants around – they were great men that time
– they prepared theirself, five or six of 'em, an' they watched him
coming back an' putting his horse an' going in an' lighting the fire.
He hung the kettle an' he prepared himself. An' they came outside
with torches an' they put 'em under the little thatched house where

he went into . Next thing was, the fire began to fall down on him an' he looked around, an' he was wondering. Now, there was a small back window an' didn't he stick his head out to escape. An' cripes, there was one lad in it with a sharp slasher an' he up with it an' hit him across the head, an' the head fell out and the body fell in.'

Gruesome stuff indeed, and in the best Carleton tradition. But if this were all there would be little reason to see it as being much different from any other nineteenth century agrarian 'outrage'. The affair need not have ended in tragedy, however. Sheehy had been warned some days previously by Biddy of the rashness of his course of action. It was his misfortune that he regarded her words as no more than an idle threat. P. Minogue continues:

'Biddy lived in the haggart where his house was an' he gave orders to her some days before that: "Biddy, you must leave here," he said. "You must leave here an' leave it soon, too. I'm going to evict all the tenants around, an' you'll be the first."

'"Take your time, now," says Biddy. "Maybe you'd go as quick yourself as I'll go."'[8]

Another account also survives, similar to this one but less gruesome, and therefore perhaps more likely to be nearer the truth:

'Oul' Sheehy, the agent, told her she should go, but she wasn't evicted at all. Biddy said "gimme a week. I'll walk out but you won't walk out when you're going.' So she went. An' they surrounded the house one night an' set fire to it an' burned him inside in it. An' he put his head out the window an' the top part of it fell down on him. An' a whitethorn grew up after an' there was a fork in it. You could put your neck into it. He was too exact. He had all the tenants around notified that he'd clear 'em out of it.'[9]

Hacked to death or smothered to death, it mattered little to Sheehy, who suffered a fate which agents knew was one of the risks of the job if they were 'too exact'.

Biddy is said to have left Ayle within days of this murder and settled in Kilbarron. Her furniture was transported by one Johnny Murphy, a chair-maker, and in payment he received what no one else ever would, a look into the famous blue bottle. It might have been better for himself if he had accepted the money which Biddy offered, for it is said by some that he became 'strange' afterwards and took to wandering away by himself.

Tulla is no more than six miles from Ayle and Biddy must have been very familiar indeed with every turn of that road. Whether she went so far as to seek work in Tulla at this time (1816-17) is another matter, but a belief persists that she did, that she came to Affick House, two miles from the village, where she worked as a parlour-maid. Mr Floyd, the present owner, tells the story:

'She was here in her youth as a parlour-maid. She lived in the locality, only two fields away from here, so it was only natural that she'd get a job here, or look for a job. It belonged to a man called Robert Spaight and he had 100 Irish acres o' land here. The place where her house was can be seen. I can show you. There's a few old whitethorns growing where it was. The shell o' the house was taken away by a man who got the bit o' land. But it was visible up to fifty years ago.

'Well, then she moved from here – the reason I can't tell you – over about a half mile the road an' she lived in another house there for a while. An' after that we lost contact with her here around. But she eventually wound up over at Kilbarron. She was young, anyway, when she was here. Oh, she was a household name around here on account o' she living in it for a while, in two houses.'[10]

This version of events is hotly denied by a man whom I interviewed in St Joseph's Hospital, Ennis:

'Where did she live in Tulla? That'll do! Listen to me! She lived in Ayle, up in Ayle, for a big number o' years, an' she lived in Kilbarron for the rest of her life. Anyone that says more than that knows nothing about her!'

Opinions differ, yet the patient lives, it seems.

It is known that she married at this time, one Pat Malley, but there is no clarity in the minds of people now living as to this. Indeed, I found in most informants almost complete uncertainty as to the actual number of her husbands (anything from two to six!), never mind their names or the order in which they were married. But mention was often made to me of her son, especially in regard to the getting of her bottle, though he is known variously as John or Pat. (This might be explained by there having been more than a single son, one subsequently confused with the other.) Other accounts have it that he was blind, though yet another says that he went to London:

'He was a great hurler but he went off to London, an' that man was never seen after that.'[11]

The two are hardly reconcilable; a blind man would hardly trade the relative security of Feakle and its environs for the hazards of a huge city like London.

Rumours were also current that he was 'carried' by the fairies, but this is of necessity difficult to verify. Whatever may have been the true facts of the case, he occupies a very minor place in the folk-memory.

A daughter is mentioned too but I collected only one story about her, though an amusing one:

'When I was in hospital in Ennis a lad was telling me a story about Biddy. His grandfather was courting the daughter, Biddy's daughter, an' in them days they were very strict on the girls – sure, my own sister, they wouldn't let her over to the pier dancing on a Sunday. But anyway, Biddy was very strict, an' he was courting her with a pounder. How could he do that? Well, a pounder is a piece of round timber they used to have that time for pounding the spuds, breaking 'em up for the pigs in the tub. I knew that, but I declare to God, I couldn't know how was he courting her with that. I was putting different meanings on it in my mind, but when the lad told me how it was, I had to laugh. His grandfather, he'd come to the house an' she wouldn't be let out, an' I s'pose the little house was a bad one – holes in the wall, or something. But whatever few times he did meet her, you see, they had a code made up, an' whatever way he'd come to the wall he'd hit the wall; whatever so many tips meant – to come out, I'll meet you on such a night or something like that. That's what it meant. I don't know what happened 'em after.'[12]

This episode, if it happened, must be assigned at the earliest to some time in the 1830s, but again, there is no way of knowing with any more accuracy.

With those few meagre details to cast a dim light on her earlier years we turn now to the question of her bottle. And what a change is there! Suddenly there is no longer a scarcity of detail; rather the opposite. The very number of theories as to how she came by it and their diversity is amazing. The story, no less than the bottle itself, obviously held a fascination for the people of her own time and for all the generations since, being second only in frequency of occurrence to the other great favourite, the story of the priest's horse (see pp.92-99).

Let us look at some of these. They provide a useful insight into the workings of the human mind in the face of the unexplained.

2: The Bottle

Everyone who has any knowledge of Biddy will have heard of her
bottle, perhaps of its colour, its size, and yet, though no one knows
quite when she came by it, practically all those I spoke to had a story
to explain how she got it. This is rather odd, even more odd when
one hears the actual explanations given for its mysterious appearance. On the face of it, practically all of them look rather unlikely.
Probably the simple truth is that since no one knew, a set of circumstances had to be invented. The following are some of the more
well-told stories:

'Biddy got married there in Carrowroe to Tom Flannery, an' they
had one son, Tom as well. An' I suppose he'd be no more than about
seven or eight years of age, the little boy, when the landlord, Colonel
Westropp-O'Callaghan, was looking for the rent. Now, Tom Flannery was dead a couple of years at this time an' sure, Biddy wasn't
able to pay it. So, she was getting letter after letter, an' visit after
visit from the police, the old RIC in Tulla, for the rent. She told 'em
that she couldn't pay it. So the next thing was, one o' the RIC men
in Tulla paid her a visit one evening an' he says to her "Well, Biddy,"
says he – he knew her – "tomorrow is your last day where you are.
You're going to be put out of it when you're not able to pay the rent."

'She went in to the fire on the way to the kitchen. The little boy
about seven or eight years of age, her son, was there an' she started
telling him about the man's visit an' that she was going to be put
out of it an' she didn't know what she was going to do or where
they were to go. But, she says to him – 'twas dusk or nightfall –
"Well, Tom," says she, "I'll go out anyway an' collect a bundle o'
rotten sticks to make a fire in the morning for our breakfast. An'
God help us, I suppose 'tis our last breakfast here in this house,
wherever we'll get it the morning after. But I'll go out anyway," says
she, "an' collect the bundle o' sticks."

'She went out, an' she wasn't gone very far when who appeared
to her only her dead husband, Tom Flannery.

'"Well, Biddy," says he to her, "I came to help you. You had a
visit from the police an' 'tisn't this visit you had at all, but many.
An' Biddy," says he, "the one that called on you today told you

you're going to be put out tomorrow. But if you do what I'll tell you now you won't be put out."

'"Well, thank you very much, Tom," says she, "an' may the Lord receive you into Heaven."

'"Say no more, Biddy," says he, "say no more, but take this bottle, this black bottle. An' every time that you look into this bottle with one o' your eyes – an' you needn't close the other one, either," says he – "every time you look into this bottle you can see what's going to happen in the future. An' Biddy," says he, "give it to nobody. Let nobody have it but yourself."

'"God bless you, Tom," says she.

'"Don't say that, Biddy," says he, "but go away an' collect your bundle o' sticks, an' bring your bottle with you. An' every time, even now, that you look into it you'll see what's going to happen. Go an' collect your bundle o' sticks now. My time is up an' I have to go."

'When he said he had to go an' handed her the bottle he disappeared. She took the bottle, anyway, collected her sticks an' brought 'em in. When she went in she said to her son:

'"D'you know who I met?" says she. "Didn't I meet daddy that's dead, an' he gave me this bottle an' he told me that I'd have enormous powers through it. An' he also told me," says she, "to take no money whatsoever, or if I did all my powers were gone an' the bottle was no good to me."

'Anyway, she looked into the bottle after leaving down her bundle o' sticks an' she saw inside in the bottle a carriage, an' a pair o' ponies being brought an' harnessed to the carriage, an' a man getting up on the high seat o' the carriage, an' another man getting into it. An' she saw police getting up on horseback an' going before the carriage along the road. An' she said to Tom:

'"Now," says she, "I've seen what's going to happen tomorrow. But I'll stop 'em."

'They went to bed an' after she going to bed Tom Flannery came back to her again, inside in the room an' he says to her:

'"Biddy," says he, "the police will lead a sheriff an' his driver tomorrow. An' when they come to the house to you all you need say," says he, "is 'Stay where you are!' They're stuck to the road. You can leave 'em there as long," says he, "as ever you like. You can leave 'em there for a month if you like. An' tell 'em when you let 'em go to trouble you no more or you'll do the same thing with 'em again."

'He disappeared. About eleven o'clock next day there did mounted police come riding, about eight of 'em, in front of a carriage an' a pair o' horses, an' a driver above in the high seat. The carriage pulled up in front o' Biddy's an' the driver came down out o' the seat. He opened the door. Biddy came out to her half-door.

'"Stay were you are!" says she to 'em. The driver couldn't walk away from the carriage. The fellow who was inside in the seat couldn't come out of it. The police couldn't come off the horses on the road.

'"I'll leave ye there, now," says Biddy, "as long as I like."

'Well, she got whatever bit she had to eat for her dinner an' for her son, Tom, an' they ate it. Biddy went off to a neighbour's house, an' she came back in the evening, got a drop o' tea, maybe for herself an' the boy. When 'twas getting dusk she came up to the door an' she says to the sheriff an' his driver an' the police:

'"Ye can go now," says she. "But don't trouble me anymore, or 'tisn't one day at all that I'll leave ye stuck to the road but several days. Go on, now while ye're able."

'Off they went an' troubled her no more.'[13]

This story contains many elements which recur again and again: the colour of the bottle (usually described as dark), instructions as to its use, a warning not to accept money, a promise of great things to come, and of course knowledge of her own power (which she was to use again in the same way against the priest on a later occasion). It is also interesting to note that Tom tells her not to mention God's blessing – a hint, perhaps, that he is in some unhallowed place. His statement 'my time is up' is reminiscent of the statement of the ghost of Hamlet's father, who has been released from otherworldly bondage to deliver a message.

During all her long life Biddy was to be plagued by this suspicion that her power was unholy, and it was to lead to much conflict with the clerical powers-that-be.

On a more immediately practical level there appears to be no mention of this episode in the police records of the time. Bureaucracy, it seems, does not allow for the otherworldly; it is not 'fact' to the official mind, therefore it does not exist. Also no policeman would find it politic to enter such an item on his report. His chances of promotion would not be enhanced thereby. Yet, it is also unthinkable that the forces of the law would allow themselves to be deflected from their purpose by a mere peasant woman. This leads us again

to the question of whether the events described actually happened
or are the figments of folk-yearnings.

Most other stories relating to how she got the bottle are fairly
evenly divided between her getting it from her son and from a
changeling in a house where she was working.

The following has a strong resemblance to the foregoing story:

'Biddy had a grand young man of a son an' he died kind o' suddenly. She was crying sitting down on the window-sill this evening.
She couldn't stop o' crying, a grand fine evening. And the sun was
on the sky all the time. An' all of a sudden he appeared before her.
An' 'twas he handed her the bottle. "I'm gone," he said, "an' I'm
safe, an' I'm happy, but this'll make a living for you instead o' me."

'An' the next thing, he was disappeared.'[14]

In this version, unlike the other, the son seems to be happy with
the state he is in, whatever it be.

The following two tellings have the son as a fiddler, and they
provide, among other details, useful comments on the powers of the
person who possessed the bottle:

'Biddy's son was blind. An' he was coming home one night from
a dance with his oul' fiddle – he used to be playing at dances – an'
begod, he met this fellow on the road, a man he knew was dead.
But the dead man was in the Good People an' he asked him to know
would he go playing for 'em at a dance they were having. So they
went into a big fort, a lios, an' the next thing was, he was playing
all night. All the people that were dancing, they were dead people,
an' one of 'em said to him, "When you're going home in the morning,
if they offer you anything to eat don't take it. An' I'll give you
something that'll be valuable to you maybe in time to come."

'So he gave him this blue bottle an' he was using the bottle while
he was alive. An' when he was dying he gave it to Biddy – that was
the mother. An' I declare to God tonight, she was using it until she
died.'[15]

Here, interestingly, we see that the son used the bottle during his
lifetime, but no known account survives of how he used it. The next
story contains nothing of this, makes him merely a messenger:

'She got her bottle from the fairies, or her son did. He was a
fiddler. He was down in Sixmilebridge an' he was coming home an'
this crowd was dancing in the road as he was coming. They were
the fairies, but he didn't think they were the fairies. He sat down –
he was a great fiddler – an' he played music with 'em. An' when

they all dispersed that was the time he realised. They all danced an'
sung, a crowd o' the smallest people he ever saw. Then they all
dispersed except one old man, an' he gave him a blue bottle an' told
him bring that home with him an' give it to his mother – she was a
widow woman at that time – but to make sure that she'd never
charge money for anything she'd do. "If she do," he said, "she'll
lose her power, but she can do anything she like with that bottle,"
he said. "She can cure anything, or tell things, or anything she want,
but tell her not to charge money. But she can take presents, an' if
she has anything left over she can distribute it to her neighbours."

'So that was that. She could put up the bottle, an' if I left home
an' went over to her she'd look into the bottle an' everything you
an' I said here she'd tell it to me.'[16]

A man from Scariff tells a slightly different version:

''Twas Biddy's son got the bottle first. He was carried by the fairies
an' he was gone twelve months. When he came back he thought he
was only gone a day, an' he got the bottle while he was there. He
came back alive an' the fairies that had him gone gave him the bottle.
But he got sick then an' was dying, so he gave it to the mother.'[17]

The impression here again is that the bottle was for his own use.
Also there is a hint that the son was a changeling.

Some stories have it that he got the bottle as a reward for help
given in a hurling match. Here is a representative example:

'She had this black bottle, you know, an' it belonged to the son.
They claim that he was a great hurler, an' these Good People, they
brought him for to play a match with 'em one night an' to recompense
him then didn't they give the bottle to him as a gift, an' they said
that'd be good for him while he'd live. But he didn't live very long
after that an' he left the bottle to the mother.'[18]

There is also a telling which ascribes the getting of the bottle not
to a son but to a brother of Biddy:

'I heard that 'twas her brother got it for doing some turn in the
night for some o' the Other Crowd. I don't know what the turn was,
but it seems he helped 'em, anyway, her brother. But he wouldn't
use it an' he gave it to her.'[19]

We come now to the other group, those tales which tell that she
got the bottle from a changeling or some related being. In the following, Biddy had been in Kilbarron only a short time, as a servant-girl
to the doctor. Frank O'Brien takes up the story:

'Doctor Dunne, he went to Scariff this Saturday, himself an' his wife. An' they had one baby about three months of age in a cot, an' Biddy was minding the baby. But she was out the back door, feeding the calves with milk, in the bucket, you know, an' she heard the music inside, the fiddle-playing. She rushed in of a sweep to know what was wrong, an' 'twas a man was in it, in the cot. An' like yourself, God bless you, he had a beard. An' he told Biddy to never give away the secret. "I'll give you a charm," he said, "that'll stay with you till you die."

'That's how she got it. But he went then, disappeared. An' she went over to put the bottle, the teat, in the child's mouth. The child was dead. He was stone dead. She got excited then an' she went for some o' the neighbours an' there did two or three o' the neighbouring women come in an' lifted him up, an' turned him this way an' that way an' every way. There wasn't a húm or a hám out of him. He *was* dead.

'She didn't know then how she'd convey the news, sure, to the doctor and the wife, an' she in charge. She was in an awful predicament. But the women stopped there till they came back from Scariff, an' one o' the women went out when they pulled in the yard with the pony an' trap, an' told 'em, that the child was dead. The doctor said nothing but herself nearly fell down. She came in, anyway, an' she looked at him an' stirred him. An' the doctor came in after, announced he was dead. Well, Biddy then had to answer, I needn't tell you, a hundred questions – what did you give him, then? Or did he swallow a shirt-button or anything? Did you give him any little didey to play with that might choke him?

'"Well, he's dead, he's dead," the doctor said. 'Twouldn't do the mother until he'd be operated on. Well, the doctor didn't want to operate on him himself, he being his own child. He sent for a doctor to Limerick an' he came the next day, a Sunday. An' they brought him over in the room, in the bed, an' this doctor from Limerick operated on him. There was nothing in the world wide inside in him to kill him, nothing that was ever known. He had nothing taken only just what he should take – that was the milk. Not a thing. He was buried then that evening, sewed up again, an' buried that evening in a *cillín*, a small graveyard for children.

'That night then, there was two o' the Kilbarron men coming down from Feakle – I suppose they had a few jars in it. An' 'twas after twelve o'clock an' "God, there's a light beyond in the *cillín*," says one of 'em. "Where?" says th' other man. "Don't you see it," he says, "the big round light?" "I don't see nothing," says th' other man. He didn't see it at all, but one of 'em saw it. Inside in the little graveyard. An' they told that around here.

'Well, that's the way she got her charm, now. 'Twas.'[20]

Thus it was that out of tragic circumstances Biddy seemed to bring the power that was to bring comfort to so many. This is an impression that is not contradicted by any of the other stories. In the following there is the added dimension of Biddy's kindness and this also is a characteristic that is apparent all through her life.

'She was in a house where there was supposed to be a changeling. That was a strange thing, how the fairies used to bring people an' leave some sort of a yoke in place o' them. Anyway, those, sure, they wouldn't be able to walk or maybe talk; you'd have to dress them an' all that, an' they'd generally die before they'd reach adulthood. But, Biddy was very nice to them an' one o' them gave her the bottle, "an' that'll make a living for you," he said. "You'll be able to tell the past, the future an' cure people of certain complaints."'[21]

A more unusual version is this one:

'Sure, they made out 'twas a fool that was in the family she got the gift from. There was a rumour about milk – he went out milking a cow an' he spilt the milk an' gother it up again an' put it into a bottle, an' 'twas out o' that the charm came.'[22]

I have collected a very similar story in Crusheen in which a dumb man who was considered a fool speaks for the first time in his life to announce the tragic death of a member of his family.

The final two stories are interesting in that they support the claim that Biddy worked in Tulla:

'When Biddy was working in Tulla there was a dwarf in the house an' when it came time for her to leave the place "Wait there," he said, an' he went up to his room an' brought down a violin. "You was very good to me," he said, "an' I might compensate you for it." An' he played the violin an' Biddy counted it great music. But he said, "I won't be long here, now." An' Biddy said "Is that the way?" "That's the way," he said. "A couple o' weeks is all I'll be in this house now. But I'll bring you something," he said, "that'll do you good."

'An' he brought her down this bottle an' he said, "That'll make a living for you, but don't leave anyone near it but yourself. An' if you want to find out anything you can look into that bottle."

'An' she got the bottle from the dwarf, but there was no power in it until the dwarf died. After that she was able to see the future in it."[23]

The other account is more straightforward:

'They say 'twas in Tulla she was when she got the bottle. She worked for nothing for this man in Tulla, an' when she was leaving he said, "Sure, I have something to give you." So she said nothing. "I'll give you what'll make a living for you," he said. He gave her the blue bottle, an' I suppose told her what she'd do with it.'[24]

There is another account, which should be quoted if only to show how anxious someone was to ascribe nobility to Biddy, nobility of ancestry as well as of motive:

'Another tradition was that she was of lady descent an' the family were dispossessed o' their land long ago. They were of the McMahons o' west Clare an' God gave her that gift to help her countrymen when they were evicted. So we don't know.'[25]

From the preceding material it may be concluded that Biddy had either got the bottle at the time of her first venturing out to work (1814-17) or by the time her son had grown up sufficiently to play the fiddle or hurl (c. 1835 – presuming that the son was of her first marriage, that of 1817). This is certainly vague, but oral tradition tells us nothing more accurate. The few other details from this period which survive relate to the bottle itself, for example, its size:

''Twas only a small little bottle, like an iodine bottle, An' she'd look into it like a crystal ball.'[26]

Its reputed colour we have heard of already, so we may pass on to a question that must have exercised the minds of all, i.e. what was in the bottle? Let P. Minogue describe it:

'When Biddy was preparing herself to go from Sheehy's place she got oul' Johnny Murphy, the chair-maker, an' she said, "Will you bring down my furniture to Kilbarron? I want to remove from here." "I will," says Johnny. "I'll bring down your furniture all right." "Do," says she, "an' I'll pay you well." "I'll want no payment, but will you gimme one look into the bottle you have." "I will," says she. "All right, so, I want no more payment."

'Begod, Biddy went in in the room an' she brought out the bottle, an' she came out an' she having it parcelled up. She caught it an' she shook it. "Look there, now," says she. A little man that was inside in it! An' if he threw himself down to die, the person who came to Biddy would die. But if he stood up straight the person'd be going out of his skin altogether. Johnny Murphy, he was the only man I ever heard tell of that looked into the bottle.'[27]

I recorded one other account which supports this in most details, and I could not help but be struck by the parallel between them and the story of Aladdin and his lamp.

When she got the bottle does not, in the final analysis, matter as much as what she was able to do with it. Some people today will say that the bottle in itself was nothing more than an aid to concentration or a prop used by Biddy to allay the fears of those who came to her – if they were convinced that her power came out of an actual object which they could see they were less likely to be frightened than if she were to work out of thin air. Perhaps she had a gift which allowed her, for example, to see and hear people at a distance, as well as into the past and future, but that is not how it comes down to us in the imagination of the people. They insist on attributing her power to the bottle:

'An' if you wanted to go to her, now, an' you were fifteen or twenty miles away from her, she could look into the bottle an' she'd know who was coming, an' she'd know what you wanted when you *would* come.'[28]

Her neighbours and those who came to her for cures *may* have been right. Maybe the bottle did have power, but if so it turned out to be a rather mixed blessing to Biddy herself for with the growth of her reputation came pilgrims bringing whiskey and poteen, among other gifts, and it was this liquor which was to play havoc with the health of two of her husbands. It also brought the wrath of neighbouring women on Biddy since they believed that their menfolk drank more free spirits than was good for them at her generous fireside. Opinions vary as to what actually happened in that kitchen, of course, as the following will show:

'All the neighbours, they'd go off in the night to Biddy an' they'd get a good mug o' whiskey – and 'twas good strong stuff. That's about all. She might give you more than one mug, but no one of 'em ever was drunk nor there was never any fighting.'[29]

Perhaps this was because Biddy took care to remain slightly aloof from the merriment:

'An' even though the house was full o' whiskey, she never drank.'[30]

Take also this next which I heard in Tulla:

'She'd take no money for her fees, but they'd leave her something, like a bottle o' whiskey. You'd get it for a shilling that time; 'twas very cheap. Well, a few men around the place would come in at night-time an' drink the bottle o' whiskey with her. Well, for that reason the parish priest in Feakle at the time condemned 'em. He made out she was a bad woman, an' that those men shouldn't go near her. An' she was supposed to get a bad name for that.'

The next account I also heard near Tulla.

'They used to come from Tipperary an' everywhere on horses an' saddles, an' in sidecars, an' every one of 'em brought whiskey. Four of her husbands died from it. An' she killed all the neighbours. All the neighbours died; they used to gather drinking this whiskey. An' she rose a lot o' disturbance in the locality, it seems, at the time. The wives were agin it, like. Their husbands went an' drank, an' came home drunk. An' they made out that the women followed her an' burned her, rose up her clothes an' burned her on the rump when she got married the fourth time. They make out that, that the women were disgusted with her.'

This latter account – which, by the way, bears a remarkable semblance to the burning of Christy Mahon in *The Playboy of the Western World* – would appear to be somewhat exaggerated, yet a similar claim of wide-ranging destruction by Biddy is to be found in Lady Gregory's account of her.[31]

The following is representative of what was said by most of those who spoke to me about her:

'What I heard 'em saying was "Anyone that ever went to her, they never came out of it dry nor hungry."'[32]

This is certainly the Biddy that the people remember. But there are those who remain unconvinced of the ultimate value of her cures:

'She might have done good for people, but it seems they were nothing in the better of it after.'[33]

Whatever of the effect, good or otherwise, of the cures on others, she herself seems to have suffered considerable hardship as a result of her mediation between two worlds:

'Oh, she used to get knocked an' tumbled inside around the house when she'd be making up the bottles for cures. An' she'd read in her bottle whether you'd be going to live or die. People went to her an' she used to put 'em out when she'd be going doctoring this bottle.'[34]

'I often heard it said that she used to get a fierce gruelling from the Good People every time she'd give out a cure.'[35]

All this lends support to the view that those who inhabit that other world give nothing for nothing and perhaps prefer to be completely

dissociated from us and our doings until forced to take a hand by
a person such as Biddy. Or could it be that they take a hand in our
affairs more often than we would care to know, and that we become
aware of this only when we have someone like her to point out to
us what we cannot see for ourselves? In the following chapter I
attempt to deal with this viewpoint.

3: A Hidden Landscape

In our day speed, machinery and the abandonment of feet as the primary means of transport have brought about a whole new way of looking (or not looking) at our physical environment. A mere generation ago every field and gap, even bushes, had a name. What, then, was the countryside like to our ancestors of the nineteenth century? In many ways it was a mysterious place though they knew it with the knowledge of men who had to pay rent for every inch of it. Dotted among their fields were forts, blessed wells, fairy hills, each with its own story passed down through the generations, a living proof that we share this ground with others who are best left alone and who occasionally need to be placated. The main problem was not what one could see – only a fool for example, would interfere with a fort – but what one might stumble across unbeknownst, in the ploughing of a field, or in the building of a house. Here lay fear, and even today stories recounting the misfortunes of people engaged in such activities are legion.

Obviously, assistance was needed if people were to live their allotted span, and luckily help was to hand in the person of the Catholic priest. There was a small problem, however: most priests were remarkably reluctant to use the power with which their people fervently invested them. This reluctance itself became a proof that 'they had the power', yet it was cold comfort to find that the priest poohpoohed the very idea of the Good People to a father or mother who knew that their child had been 'carried' by Them. Naturally, people turned to where they would receive a hearing, and Biddy's door was always open.

Whether she really did see into another world, or whether she merely observed this one more closely than her contemporaries is not likely ever to be known, but what is not in doubt is that she brought consolation to many through offering them an explanation of their problems often in terms of their natural surroundings. Of course, what soon strikes the observer in all these cases is the uncanny knack she had of knowing what each one was suffering from as well as why, and her ability to name them and where they had come from before ever they had opened their lips.

There was more to her than mere observation or native shrewdness could explain. It was this which brought an ever-growing flood of visitors to her door, each with his or her own tale of woe. Let us look at some of these visitors and the landscape to which they owed their ills: .

'This man, he had land in the parish of Corofin, an' there was a well in it an' a boreen down to it. One day he went down an' he cleared around the well, cut back the blackthorns an' things out of it. He was doing that for no harm to anyone, only to make it handy for getting at the well. But 'tis never right to cut any bushes around a spring well an' 'twas he proved the truth o' that, because he got the pain, an' bad. Now, there was no doctors that time for the likes o' him, a poor man, so as soon as he got the pain his neighbours told him:

'"Oh, the fairies'll have you gone. Go to Biddy Early, quick."

'So off to Biddy with him. . . Is it right to say "The Lord have mercy on her", d'you think? Well, I think 'tis. . .

'But he went up anyway an' he said he had an awful pain in his side there an' could she do anything?

'"I can," she said, "but you have to do something for me."

'"Oh, whatever it is I'll do it for you."

'"Will you keep away from that well that you cut the bushes in," says she. "An' that boreen, once every twelve months is enough to go down there. Go home now, an' when you'll get a bowel motion," she said, "have a look out."

'So he did. An' what did he find only two inches an' a half of a thorny piece o' blackthorn. That's what was causing the pain. But 'twas from interfering with the well he inherited it. He didn't swallow it. So they can do them things, the Good People. An' there's something in a spring well! You aren't supposed to touch anything around it, or refuse anyone for water. 'Twas put there by someone, but it wasn't put there by you.'[36]

That there was 'something in a spring well' is well attested to by the number of blessed wells that survive even today; scarcely a parish in Ireland is without one. But in Biddy's time, before the advent of pumps and piped water a good spring was of understandable importance and great care had to be taken to protect the supply. Much May Day lore centres on the well, and so Biddy was impinging on the deepest sensitivities of her people when her advice touched on spring water. Take the following, for example:

'My grandfather, he lived in Inagh an' in the meadow this day they went up to call a man that was working in it. An' he was lying over in the hay. He was gone a bit feverish so they brought him in home. They brought a doctor to him but the doctor didn't know what was wrong, an' that time a lot of people'd swear that Biddy was better than any doctor. But, my grandfather took off on horse-back – an' he was a fair good man to ride a horse – an' off to see Biddy. An' he pulling up at the house, she came out to the door an' she said,

'"I know what brought you here. My dear man," she said, "your friend is very sick."

'"He is," said my grandfather.

'An' she went in an' she brought out this bottle.

'"There's three spring wells," she says, "in that man's land, an' before the sun rises in the morning have some out o' that bottle put into the three spring wells, an' he'll get all right. An' when you're going, now," she says, "there's such a cross, be careful at that cross, because the horse'll run you."

'An' he came to the cross an' the horse stood, an' then bolted. Well, he held on to him – he was a good man on the horse – an' brought him an' went home, told 'em at home what to do with the bottle. They did, an' in about a week he was all right.'[37]

The messenger might have been less confident in facing Biddy for a cure for his friend had he known of her usual reaction to those who had engaged the services of a doctor before coming to consult her. But in this case the patient was lucky; Biddy seems not to have made an issue of it.

In the next story the spring water itself is given to the messenger and acts effectively against the Good People:

'There did a family live in Cooleen Bridge above Scariff – 'twould be on the road, now, from Scariff to Whitegate an' Mountshannon. But, one of 'em, Paddy, got sick, an' his brother John went over to Kilbarron – he had only about a mile to go – over to Biddy to know could she cure Paddy. An' when he went over she was inside at home.

'"Muise, Johnny," says she, "your brother is beyond in bed sick, an' you came over to me to know could I cure him. Begod, I will, Johnny," says she, "but wait here until I come in. I must go out for a bottle. An' to tell you the truth, Johnny, a bottle o' water out o' the well is what I'm going to give you. An' 'twill cure him. But," says she, "'tis what's making you brother sick now are the fairies.

An' I'm going to clear the fairies with this bottle o' spring water out o' the well. Take that bottle home," says she. "Bring it *quick* home an' give him a mouthful of it."

'She came back, anyway, an' she handed him about a pint bottle full o' well water.

'"Take that home now," says she, "as fast as ever you can. An' when you go in to your brother get him to take a mouthful of it immediately. And, don't let him take any more until the same time tomorrow. An' don't let him take only another mouthful of it then, an' the same the day after, at the same time. An' when he takes the third mouthful out of it, what's left in the bottle, have a good fire down in the kitchen an' throw the remainder of it," says she, "into the fire, when you'll get a surprise. An' make sure that the kitchen door an' the kitchen window are open. If they're not you'll suffer, an' your brother will suffer."

'So he took the bottle anyway an' as quick as ever he could went back to Cooleen Bridge. He went back, an' into the room where his brother was in bed. An' his brother Paddy rose it on his head, the bottle. He took a mouthful o' the water an' after he taking it he got a fit o' shivering, an' he was shivering like a lump o' jelly in a plate. He was that way all day an' that way all night an' next day, until the following evening at the same time that he took another mouthful o' the bottle. Then the shivering stopped. But he never slept after taking the second mouthful o' the bottle. He got up that night. He was going around the house all night an' he couldn't get to bed, nor he couldn't go to bed the next day. An' when his brother John gave him the third mouthful o' the bottle he went into bed, covered himself up, an' John went out to the kitchen. An' there was a good fire down in the kitchen. He threw the remainder o' the water into the fire, an' 'twas a fire o' turf an' sticks that was in the kitchen. Now, as you know, if you throw water into a turf fire or a stick fire 'tisn't smoke that'd rise out of it but white steam. Well, it wasn't steam that rose out of it only hundreds upon hundreds of. . . they were like crows that flew out o' the fire. An' only for he having the window o' the kitchen open an' the door open they'd fill the house, the things like crows'd fill the house. But, they went out the door an' out the window.

'John, anyway, went back that evening to Biddy an' he told her what happened.

'"I told you," says she, "that 'twas the fairies that were making him sick, an' I put the fairies away from him. An' when you threw what was in the bottle into the fire you put the fairies going from him. An' when you go back home, now," says she, "your brother Paddy will be as well as ever he was. An' only for me the fairies'd have him taken."'[38]

It is not difficult, in cases like this, to see why 'They' might be angry with Biddy and even beat her. After all, she had just foiled their plans for a new acquisition of human flesh and blood.

But all of Biddy's attentions were not devoted to the otherworldly attributes of wells. On occasion, she could harness the very flow of the water itself, and for practical purposes, as this story shows:

'My father an' his brother, they were both going to school this morning when they see Biddy's house lighting. So they ran down to help to quench it, or to examine it. All the old men gathered to quench the fire an' they had all the things left out – pictures an' whiskey an' all kinds of everything. But they had no fire-brigade, an' there was only a small well below the house. They drew the water with buckets, the older men, an' threw it up on the little thatched house. But the fire was beating 'em an' they came back an' they said:

'"Biddy, we'll have to resign. There's no more water in the well."

'"Oh, God," says she, "is that the way?"

'She put on her apron and went down, an' whatever she said or done around the well, the water flowed out an' ran down the road in a minute. So the old men continued an' put out the fire.'[39]

At wells, which were a focus-point for both the Good People and ordinary mortals there might be some excuse for occasional friction, but anyone mad enough to interfere with a fort might expect certain retribution. A brief example will suffice from the hundreds on record:

'This fellow was rooting a fort an' a blackthorn – 'twas all blackthorn – it picked him there in the knee. An' the knee couldn't get better. In the finish he was brought to Biddy. An' she looked at him, an' she told him where it happened an' why it happened.

'"I'll cure you," says she, "but go! Or they'll get you again."'[40]

Many such disturbers of the abodes of the Good People never knew a day's peace again until they crossed flowing water to England or America, thereby escaping the fairy wrath.

Another hazardous enterprise was the extension of a house to the west. It is summed up well in the following maxim:

'"'Tis a man stronger than God that builds on the west end of his own house." That was an old saying in Irish around here.'[41]

The belief was widespread that bad luck would follow such build-ing, that the extra room would be in the way of 'Them', an echo, it seems, of some early, pre-Christian mythology which saw the west, the domain of the setting sun, as the Land of the Dead. What might happen to the foolhardy builders is clearly demonstrated in this piece:

'Listening to the old people, the verdict that they always had was "never build to the western side".

'There was a house in Ballinruan, an' they built a room to the western side of it, an' everything was going on, noise, an' things falling. So they went to Biddy, an' she told 'em they had it built on the fairies' path, to go home an' knock it. "An' build at the other side," she said, "an' ye'll do."

'An' it happened. They did, an' they had no more trouble.'[42]

But the Good People could be reasonable, too, as if they recognised that a genuine error might be made and were anxious to make up any loss caused by the effects of human ignorance. Johnny Broderick explains:

'There was a house over in the village an' there was a little shed there one time at the west end o' the house, a shed with a galvanised roof. An' I never saw it only with the galvanised thrown up on it. 'Twouldn't be nailed at all. The wind might knock it an' 'twould be thrown up simple again. 'Twas never kept in any repair, that oul' shed. But, when they used to buy pigs an' put 'em in there, they'd be found dead, black. Anyhow, a few rounds o' them died an' the man who owned it, he said he'd go out to Biddy. And he did. He told her the story.

"Well," she says, "that's our path at the end of that house. An' I'm sorry," she says, "that your pigs had to die. But I'll tell you what you'll do. Never put a pig there again. Make another little house on the other side o' the yard, or anywhere at all, an' the ones you'll put in it'll make up for the ones that died."

'And they did. They throve the finest, the next set o' pigs or two that was put in the new building. But never again was there a hand left to that oul' shed.'[43]

In this account, note that Biddy calls the path 'ours', a hint that she was indeed 'in the fairies'.

If the builders persisted in ignoring continuing warning-signs, then the consequences for the family could be tragic, as they would surely have been in the next account but for the advice of Biddy:

'People here above, they was building an addition to the house. O' course, we always heard you should never build anything at the western side of your house. But they was building this room, anyway, to the western side an' they had it fit for to roof. Now, they had three or four childer, an' the childer got sick. An' they was getting worse an' worse, right bad. The doctors was coming but they couldn't do anything with 'em, an' someone said to the man to go over to Biddy, to see what she had to say. He went over.

'"Oh, go home," she says, "an' knock that room, them walls you're putting up. That's the fairies' path. If you don't do that," she said, "your childer'll be dead before this day week."

'So he came home an' he knocked his room, left 'em their path. The childer was all right in two days. There was no more about it.'[44]

The taboo on building to the west was at least clear and of long standing, but what about fairy paths in other less conspicuous places? Hard and painful experience seems to have been the order of the day, as the following suggests:

'Down near my own place a fellow was planting whitethorns just to make fencing, but his cattle got sick after he planted a certain spot an' he could get no reason for it, so he went to Biddy Early. She said not to plant the whitethorns there any more, that they were in the path o' the fairies. So he put a sally tree in it instead, an' 'tis there yet.

'Seemingly they have feeling in 'em. They'd tear themselves passing, you see. So there must be a certain amount o' natural life in 'em then, you'd imagine.'[45]

The next story suggest the same:

'There was another family – they're gone now – an' they had fairies. The cups an' saucers an' everything used be taken out, an' all the míle murder used be happening around the house. An' they went to Biddy, an' she told 'em that they had the path destroyed on Them; they were throwing out the nuisance (rubbish) o' the house down on top o' their path.

'"If ye don't stop that, they'll take the house over entirely on ye. They'll put ye out of it clear an' clean. But if ye throw that nuisance at th' other side o' the house," says she, "ye'll be all right."

'An' so they did, an' there was no more about it. She knew all them things. She knew where the path was an' she knew where They were going an' what was happening. There was no question about that.'[46]

Sometimes the Good People's domain might be impinged on without the person's being any the wiser as to why, even when he went
to Biddy for advice:

'Here below there's the shell of an oul' house. An' an oul' man
an' woman lived in it one time. An' they pulled shrubs below the
back gate in that oul' wooded place. The man got sick so someone
advised the wife to go to Biddy. An' Biddy told her that if she put
back what he took out o' the plantation he'd get better. They did
bring it back, an' he got all right.'[47]

Health rather than explanations was foremost in people's minds
at such times of crisis, no doubt.

One other activity that could bring conflict with 'Them' was land
reclamation. To the nineteenth century smallholder plots of land
that would today be ignored made the difference between survival
and starvation, so it is not surprising that men were tempted to
reclaim even marginal land. But such places, undisturbed through
the ages and so appropriated by the Good People for their own
mysterious purposes, could hold ugly surprises for the enterprising
farmer, as this account shows:

'There was a man in this village an' he had a garden up in a place
called *Cúinne Bhéicí*. An' there were two stones in the middle o' the
garden an' when he'd be digging he'd be going in too tight on 'em.
But this little girl, his daughter, she got sick an' he went down to
Biddy Early. That time, God help us, you'd be gone walking down
to Feakle maybe a day an' a night. An' when he was going in the
avenue she knew what was wrong, that he was a case for her. But
if you weren't she'd tell you. Now, Biddy told him:

'"For goodness sake," she said, "why don't you put a bit o' clay
up with those stones in your garden instead o' taking it away from
'em! Why're you so stingy?"

'An' she was never up this way in her life! Wasn't that strange?
Oh, he went home, did what she told him. An' the girl got better.
An' the stones are still there. 'Twas a garden then but 'tis a meadow
now. They might be shelter for Those People, the Good People, you
see.'[48]

Sometimes the warning was visited on the person himself. Here
again the guidance of Biddy was invaluable. Only she could tell
whether the harm done was irreparable or otherwise:

'My great-grandfather lived only a mile from here, an' in idle times
or when he hadn't very much to do, he was rooting bits o' ground.

All he had was four an' a half acres o' land an' he was levelling it out – an oul' stone here an' there, he'd dig a hole an' bury em, an' all this. But he was at these stones, anyway, an' he had two of 'em rose an' buried, an' he was working at the third one when he got a violent headache, so bad so that he had to go home. His home wasn't very far, about a half mile. So he sat in a chair when he went home an' after a start he went to bed to rest the head. Three days, anyway, elapsed an' the headache was still there. So he knew Biddy, an' he said he'd go to her. She had a name that time for being able to cure. So he went to her in his ass an' car, an' o' course the minute he knocked at the door she opened it an' she knew him. They chatted away. Sure, she asked for everyone around Tulla that she knew, an' after a start he told her about his headache. An' she said that she'd see. So she went into the room – the room, now, was off o' the kitchen – an' when she came out again,

'"Well, Mick," says she, "you're a lucky man. Had you rooted the third stone," says she, "I could have done nothing for you. An' go home now," says she. "You'll be all right. An' have nothing to do with them. They're playing around them stones in the evening," she says, "before dusk."

'That was the Good People. But, he came home an' he was all right. I couldn't vouch for the story I'd hear from another, but that's no hearsay. That happened.'[49]

There is a suggestion here that Biddy went into the room to consult her bottle. We can also see that her power was limited. This will appear again shortly and in more definite examples.

But it was not only the Good People one had to contend with. The spirits of the departed had to be treated with due consideration, and there were always the shapeless terrors that lurked outside the four walls of the house, anxious to gain entry if allowed. Biddy had advice to impart on all such matters, as this piece from Doolin shows:

'A man from here went down to Biddy for a cure for a young daughter that was sick at home. She was delicate, you know. He got this bottle from her an' he was coming away.

'"Wait a minute," she said, "You have a broken glass in your window. An' for God's sake, wouldn't you put a small bit o' glass in it. 'Twouldn't cost you much an' it could save you a lot. An' tell that little girl not to be staying by the fire at night."

'You know, it wasn't a nice thing to be up by the fire at night. They say the old people on the other side, the people that's gone, might like to be around the fire after a certain hour themselves, talking about the old times, I suppose.'[50]

From Kilkishen, on the other side of County Clare, we have a similar belief in the dangers of unglazed windows:

'My grandfather – he's buried since 1912 – he went to see Biddy. He went with a neighbour just for company. What was wrong with the neighour I never heard. But, they went in to Biddy, talked to her, an' the next thing, she says,

'"You're living in a house under the hill."

'"I am," he says.

'She knew their names as well.

'"Listen to me," she says. "On the western side o' the house there's a bedroom, an' there's a garret over it."

'"There is," he says.

'"An' out o' that garret," she says, " there's a hole in the wall out into a cow-house, an' there's no glass in it. If you take my advice," she says, "go home an' put a glass an' a window in that. That's a very unlucky thing." But, until ten or twelve years ago that window was up there. A square hole that was there before that an' the window was only tacked up against the wall, just a temporary job for the purpose.'[51]

In spite of her general willingness to be helpful there were nonethe-. less cases in which Biddy could do nothing, either because the injury inflicted on the Good People was of an unforgivable kind, or because she was facing beings whose malignant power she could not deflect. In the first of the following, misfortune could easily have been avoided whereas in the second it is hard to see how the victim could have escaped:

'My grandfather, he rooted a fort an' at the time his sister was a teacher out in the County Galway. An' she got sick, so he went to Biddy Early, you see. An' Biddy told him that 'twas he was the cause of it.

'"There's a Fool among the fairies," she said, "an' she's struck by the Fool o' the fairies, an' I don't think I can do anything for her. But you're the cause of it. You rooted the fort," she said, "at the back o' the house across the road from you."

'But she died, anyway. You see, there's a Fool among the fairies, an' if he just touches, nothing can be done. If 'twas any other one of 'em, it seems, she could do something.'[52]

Reference is made to this Fool by Carolyn White in her book on

Irish fairies.[53]

'There was another man I used hear 'em talking about out the mountain there in front of where I come from, Kilmurry. He got stung with a bee an' he went to her an' she cured him. But the bee came about in twelve months time and stung him again. So he went again to her. But she told him that she could do nothing for him, that 'twas the Coolmeen Lake witch that stung him.'[54]

Who this witch was I have not been able to discover, nor is it clear why she should have singled him out for such treatment. And why was Biddy able to cure him once but not a second time? Intriguing echoes here, indeed.

In conclusion to this section, it may be said that Biddy was a conservative force; conservative in the sense that she reminded people of their duty to a world they could not see and were therefore liable to forget on occasion. But she was also a reassuring figure, explaining, warning or criticising where necessary, someone to whom people could and did turn when their actions brought inexplicable reactions, when life seemed to be going against them in ways that defied reason. In an age more vivid in its beliefs than ours she served the useful and worthy purpose of spiritual lightning-rod, taking the worst sting out of otherworldly blasts in all but a few cases and enlightening many people in the process.

4: All God's Creatures

The strange notion that wild creatures are for the use and pleasure of mankind, are to be killed or let live to convenience humans, is one that is still very much with us. That they might be entitled to go about their own business would seem odd even to many twentieth century people. The idea of protecting species *per se* is gaining only slow acceptance whereas protection with an ulterior motive has been in the world a long while, for example, carefully nurturing pheasants so that they may be shot later at leisure by a select group. In our society, where there is no longer any primary need for the common man personally to do the killing there is less excuse for such behaviour than there might have been in a time and place when food needed to be taken as opportunity offered. And so it is all the more surprising to find, in the various accounts of Biddy Early's doings, that her attitude to animals wild or domestic was an enlightened and rational one. She did not, except in rare and justifiable occasions, place them on a level with humans, but neither did she use them in a cruel or degrading manner.

In that rural nineteenth century society, animals were more immediate and intimate neighbours than they now are, and of far more importance to the average person. Many of the small household items which marked the bounds between mere existence and frugal comfort were acquired as a result of the housewife's skill with hens and geese. The loss of a pig or calf could mean the difference between payment and non-payment of rent on gale-day. The death of a working-horse could spell destitution. In such a society, therefore, it comes as no surprise that many of the queries brought to Biddy's door related to the health and welfare of such animals, all the more so when vets and medicines as we understand them were more than half a century in the future.

Familiarity bred contempt, too, of course, and there is much evidence of vile cruelty to animals in that age, but none of it touches Biddy. In my collecting I have come across no story, however small, that could be used to point an accusing finger at her in this regard, and one only in which she actually harms a person to benefit an animal. More about that case later (p. 56-7).

One might account for her benevolent attitude in two ways: firstly, by accepting that that was her nature; secondly, by claiming that she was aware of the otherworldly connections of some animals and therefore respected them – as, indeed, people in general did. These latter would include the horse and the hare particularly, both of them receptive to movement from the unseen world.

The truth probably lies somewhere between the two views. That she was of a kind, open, generous nature is attested to by the following:

'Without a doubt, she never did only a good turn to someone'.[55] 'Oh she was a very nice little woman to go in to, very friendly, an' 'tis unknown what presents she used to get'.[56] 'That woman divided chickens – she might often get ten chickens in the day, an' she'd divide 'em out and' give 'em to the neighbours. Amn't I telling you! She could be a millionaire. But what I'm coming at, while there was no money into the bottle, an' she was able to do anything with it, she fed the neighbours round her'.[57]

Her friendliness to children also is seen in this story:

'She was counted always a good Christian. She never took money, only loaf bread an' jams or whatever anyone'd bring like that. Young people, if they was around, she'd give 'em cuts of loaf bread an' jam, an' 'twas a great rarity that time. My grandfather an' his brother, the morning they went down, that the house was on fire, she cut big cuts of a loaf an' put a big coat o' jam on 'em'.[58]

Though I have come across no mention of her having a cat – which might seem strange to many people, considering that she was so widely regarded as a witch – she kept a dog, or dogs, as these short pieces show:

'I often heard about Spot, some dog named Spot she had one time. He used to go with messages. She could put an oul' stocking around his neck an' she'd send him off, an' she was abe to direct him with the bottle – radio-control, nearly.'[59]

'My grandfather, he was a great man for the beagles, an' they were out one day an' they chased a hare into a ditch. Well, they levelled the ditch, almost, looking for him, but no sign of him. They were near Biddy's house so my grandfather went over to her, told her the problem. She came out an' a small dog behind her.

'"Go down there, Fedel," she says, "an' put him out."

'Off he went an' in no time at all he had the hare put running.

'"What kind o' huntsmen are ye at all?" says she, an' she left 'em there'.[60]

I was most surprised to hear of this strange name on the dog, but Mrs Sheehan, who told me the story, was adamant:

'That fellow Castro, that's in charge of Cuba, Biddy's dog had the same name as him.'

In the previous piece the idea of Biddy's watching over the dog by means of the bottle need not be seen as merely quaint or humorous. We shall see in chapter 6 how her ability in this respect was, for those who called on her, one of the more unnerving features of her power.

The above mention of the hare leads me to two further stories involving this animal, one treating it as an ordinary beast, the other as not quite so ordinary:

''Twas a St Stephen's Day, an' these two men came up from the Mills, up by the Black Sticks, up to where Biddy lived. An' she was standing in the road.

'"Ye're like men," she said, "that'd be going hare-hunting."

'"The very thing, then, an' we didn't meet a thing from here to the Mills."

'"Now," she pointed down towards Kilbarron lake.

'"Put the dogs in there," says she, "an' I'll bet anything that they'll rise a hare in it."

'An' they were no sooner inside when they rose a hare. Out he came on the road, an' the two hounds an' a terrier after him. Up the road with him, an' on for Feakle, on up by Kilclaran an' Caher, Doogloun, Kilanena, Drumandoora, an' straight down into the Grand Gate in Lough Cutra, Gough's place. Well, there was a roundabout there an' the hare turned there an' the hounds after him, an' back again the same road, right back the whole way. An' Biddy was still standing in the road, an' the two men with her.

'"They're coming now," says she, "an' they have a good hunt behind 'em."

'So Biddy stretched out her apron an' the hare jumped into it.

'"Go home now, do ye," says she. "Ye had a good hunt. They're after doing thirty-six miles now."

'"How do you know that?" says one of 'em.

'"I *do* know it," says she. "They're after going to the Grand Gate. An' 'tis eighteen miles from here to there, an' eighteen more back, an' what is that? 'Tis thirty-six miles."

'Now, there was no ointment that time in chemists' or anywhere, you know, an' she brought up the hare, an' in the hole here in the arch o' the fire she had goose-grease. You know, when you'd kill a goose, you'd have th' oul' fat. She rubbed that to the hare's paws, an' let him off down in over the wall again, into the fána. Wasn't that good? She done that, then.'[61]

Here, it seems almost as if Biddy was keeping the hare for some such eventuality and the fact that she puts it back into the same place after the chase suggests that it will be needed again at some future date. That she knew the exact circuit without benefit of bottle points to her having gone through the ritual previous to that.

The next story sees the hare in a much more familiar light, as the innocuous animal form of a human enchanter:

'Long ago, you see, the butter used to be taken – an' that was a fact! Now, this man in Glandree, he had six cows, five an' a Kerry cow. But he had no butter. He was churning an' churning but 'twas only whey was in it, only froth. So he went down to Biddy, an' she knew what was wrong with him the minute he was coming in the yard at Kilbarron. She lived there, you know, in a thatched house. So he told her. She asked him first had he a shotgun. He said he had.

'"Well," she said, "May Eve, watch your cows all night. An' there will a hare come down through the fields an' suck the Kerry cow. An' when you'll see that, shout," she said, "an' the hare'll run away. But don't shoot that hare in the head, the body or any place high. Shoot down low an' you might get in a few grains in the legs. An' the hare," she said, "will hop out over the wall above at the road, an' cross the road, an' go in through a window into a house."

'An' the hare did do that. Everything like Biddy said.

'But the man was very excited all night, an' he told his wife, an' he went out in the morning then for the cows, an' up to the road an' had a look across to the house. An' there was a horse an' saddle tied to the gate, a good horse, you know, an' a new saddle. Anyone around there hadn't a saddle like it. 'Twas the doctor, taking out the pellets out o' this woman's leg. 'Twas a woman that turned herself into a hare. She was bringing the butter – an' bringing it all round the area. An' she had tubs o' butter in Feakle every Thursday. But it stopped after that.

'He milked the cows then, churned, an' he had the churn full o' butter. He went down in his horse an' car to thank her, an' to pay her. She'd take no money.

'"No, but I'll tell you what you'll do," says she. "Bring me down a print o' that nice butter you have."

'An' he did. An' brought her down a half a pan of it. He had butter then from that over.'[62]

This is surely one of the best-known of Irish tales. In the age before creameries, the age of home-churning and butter-making, the wealth of many farming families lay in their cows and precautions had to be taken to protect the butter against evilly-disposed neighbours and others at all times, but especially on May Eve, one of the crucial changing-times of the pagan year, a time when the barrier between our world and the other was at its thinnest. (For a detailed description of these precautions see K. Danaher's *The Year in Ireland*.[63]) Biddy would have been even more sensitive than her contemporaries to such matters, so it is no surprise, in this case at least, to find that her attitude was one of respect for the animal – or was it for the person? – even though her solution to the problem of the butter-stealing was a drastic one.

But in that most popular of all tales relating to her, the sticking of the priest's horse to the road, where one would expect to find her treatment of the animal influenced by her attitude to the man, I have, out of thirty-two renderings of the story, come across only one version where the matter is even alluded to. It is this:

'The parish priest in Feakle then was cursing her off o' the altar an' giving her a woeful hand, ordering the people not to be paying heed to her; that they shouldn't be listening to her at all. He was terrible bad to the people to be going to her for cures or for anything. But this day he was out with his horse, driving down Coolrea an' the horse took fright an' went into a big trench. An' he got what men was around Feakle an' they couldn't bring the horse out of it, twenty or thirty men on the road. No hope o' pulling the horse up. But one oul' man that was in it, he went to him an' he says:

'"Father," he says, "what about Biddy Early?"

'"I don't like her," he says.

'"Whatever about liking her, maybe she'd do something for the horse."

'"Ah," he said, "have a try."

'But the man went.

'"By God," says Biddy, "it took him a long time to give you consent for to come."

'"It did," said the oul' man, "but he has a fine horse. Maybe you'd be abe to do something for him."

'"Well, even that he cursed me itself," she said, "'tis the horse I have compassion for. Go back," she says, "an' take the bridle yourself, an' tell them men to keep out o' your way. Give it a shake, an' tell him to get up out o' there."

'Went back, done it, an' the horse jumped on the bank, up on the road. An' from that day to the day he left Feakle he never said a word to Biddy again. That finished it.'[64]

This, by itself, is hardly enough to prove that Biddy had a high regard for horses, since it is likely that if the priest had been riding on a badger she would have expressed a similar preference, given the agitated state she was then in. Also it may merely reflect the sensibilities of the teller. But in any case I let it speak for itself. In chapter 7, as we shall see, the priest rather than the horse cringes in the limelight, a position he would gladly have traded with the animal.

There is one other tale – a tale of a tail, one might call it – which is often told about Biddy, but it fits into the category of the 'Clare will never win another Hurling Final until. . .' story. That is, it has attached itself to Biddy in the way foretold by Lady Gregory. I have collected versions of it in west Limerick and in Kerry, and in none of them is there any mention of Biddy. Here, howerver, is the Clare version:

'There did a man from Flagmount, he went down to the Bridge for pigs – there used to be fairs them times. He went down to buy three slips, an' he bought 'em. But they had no transport in them times, an' a pig, you know, is a very bad walker. He was coming back by Feakle, back by Kilbarron, walking his pigs, an' sure the three of 'em gave up in the road down below Biddy's a small bit. There was a house on the side o' the road by the name o' Gleeson's an' he went in, to know was there any place he'd put up the pigs for the night. Sure, no one had a cabin them times, unless a small little cabin for a cow an' an ass, so the man told him "would you go up there," he said, "to Biddy Early. She's only a few yards up the road there. An' go up an' in. She might do something for you."

'Up goes the man in to Biddy an' –

'"God, my poor man," she said, "your pigs are down" – without he saying anything at all.

'"Indeed they are," he said, "down there below in the road, an' they aren't able to get up."

'"Ah," she says, "sit down an' have a cup o' tea. They'll be all right."

'Sat down, an' she made tea for him an' they talked.

'"I'll do something for you, anyway," she said. "I'll help you out."

But, after a while, when he had the tea drank, he rose up, an' she gave him three pills, three middling small ones – they could be pieces o' paper but it wouldn't matter. Anything she'd give him would right the thing, whatever it was. Then she gave him another one for himself. She was gone in in the room while he was drinking the tea, making up this stuff for him.

'"When you go down, now, rise up the pigs' tails," she says, "an' put one each up under their tails. An' maybe," she says, "at the next turn o' the road you might have to let down your pants an' do the same job."

'But when they were going round the turn o' the road, the three pigs started to fly! He hardly got time to let his trousers down to have the operation. An' the four of 'em ran it to Flagmount. Never pulled up until the four of 'em landed above in Flagmount, flying!

'So that was Biddy Early for you, hah!'[65]

True or not, the story matches others in its presentation of Biddy as the friendly and hospitable helper of those in distress, and adds what is rarely otherwise seen in her character, an earthy sense of humour. If she did, in fact, behave in so uninhibited (for those times) a manner it could provide one more clue as to why she scandalised the more pious in her locality and made inevitable the clashes with the clergy which were to be a recurrent feature of her later years.

Finally, we can reasonably say, from the material available, that Biddy in her outlook on animals was conventional, though perhaps more enlightened than most of her contemporaries towards the wild and domestic creatures that shared the same countryside as human beings. Her view was hierarchical in that she saw animals occupying a place below the human – the many examples of her transferring a human ailment on to an animal, or her making an animal pay in some way for a human cure, are evidence of this. But there is never a hint, at least in so far as I am aware, of her showing deliberate cruelty to any beast. The same impression comes across from the vast majority of her dealings with people, thereby lending credence to the view of her that survives: kind though not flattering, helpful insofar as she was able, and well disposed towards creatures large and little.

5: To Cure or Not to Cure

The vast majority of the hundreds of stories and anecdotes about
Biddy that I have collected over ten years deal with two aspects of
her career, her cures and her foretelling of the future. In this chapter
I deal with the first of these.

If, with the benefit of more scientific knowledge, greater hygiene
and access to a reasonable medical service, people today are as prone
to physical and mental ailments as ever, then it must not be wondered
at that in the nineteenth century Biddy and *mná feasa* like her should
have been the first recourse of multitudes. Doctors were at a premium
and in many cases beyond the resources of the peasantry. On the
other hand Biddy's door was open to all who genuinely wished for
a cure. The tendency was to go to her first. This became more imperative when word spread that she objected to treating those who had
come to her only after seeing priest or doctor beforehand. She obviously took pride in her skills and gift and was therefore prepared to
play second fiddle to no one. But there was something else. By coming
to her first the suppliant displayed faith in her power, and it was
this faith more than anything else that guaranteed the cure.

Many and varied must have been the emotions of those who
approached her house – confidence, trepidation, downright fear –
but the very act of coming was a step nearer peace of mind, and
perhaps of body, too. That thousands did come is beyond doubt, as
these accounts tell us:

"'Twas abroad she figured right high, with people coming from
Limerick, Tipperary an' Galway as well as a good part o' Clare to
see her."[66]

Johnny Broderick, of Derrybrien, Co. Galway, spreads her catch-
ment area even wider:

'They was coming from all over Ireland. They was coming from
Cork, Kerry, all the south, an' down here, all Connaught especially,
as well as over Tipperary an' on over to Kilkenny. As far as that.'

'My father was going to Limerick one time, an' from the bridge
here below, Biddy Early's bridge, from that to above the house, there
was nothing only oats along the side o' the road – scattered with all
the horses.'[67]

"'Tis horses and' cars they'd have in them days, an' any time there'd
be a row of 'em going the road, people'd be saying "Oh, them are
off to Biddy Early's." '[68]

It is said that even English visitors came to her, and those of no
low degree, either:

'Sure, they came from England to her. Didn't one o' the royal
family come over one time to be cured, that there was something
wrong with her. She came over on the quiet, they say.'[69]

There is no record of whether this personage was cured or not,
but it is probably a fair commentary on Biddy's art that no more is
known of the incident. Publicity obviously played little part in the
way she operated. Since she was not seeking fame or personal gain
she took each visitor as she found him/her – as a person – without
regard for such superficialities as wealth or rank. In our day it is
almost unthinkable that such a visit would not be used to the full
for public relations purposes.

To the troubled visitor Biddy's manner and looks would have
been reassuring:

'She was an ordinary little farmer's wife. She was small, but a
good-looking little woman.'[70]

But this was still the moment of truth: should a gift be offered
first, or would it be better to explain one's case and leave remuner-
ation until later? As it happened, Biddy in most cases did the intro-
ducing and in a way which visitors found extremely unnerving. She
could tell them who they were and what their business was if she
chose to do so. A large number of the stories I have heard contain
this episode, no doubt because it created such a strong impression
on the minds of callers and those to whom they told their exploits.
I have already mentioned in the introduction my own experience in
this regard, and I can vouch for the vividness of the impression that
remains even yet.

Biddy's first words might raise or dash the hopes of the visitor,
but that was up to her. There is no escaping the fact that she was
in charge and that what she said was final.

In general it may be said that in the whole matter of cures there
were basically two choices. First choice was Biddy's – to cure or not.
Second choice was the sufferer's – to be cured or not.

As has been hinted at already, she could choose not to cure for a
variety of reasons: (a) if one had already visited priest or doctor, or
otherwise displayed lack of belief in her power (b) if she considered

the ailment as not coming within the domain of her power (c) if the suppliant had displeased her in some way, for example, by speaking slightingly of her or her power.

It might seem odd to suggest that the suppliant had a choice of being cured, since the very act of coming to her would seem to prove that such a choice had already been made. But examples will be quoted to show that in some cases it was only when Biddy spelt out the options that a hard, sometimes almost impossible, choice had to be made (see p. 60), a proof, perhaps, of the hidden ramifications of seemingly simple acts. In very many cases, too, there was a test of sorts to be endured, probably to find out whether or not the person wanted the cure badly enough. The most common form of this test occurred on the way home, when Biddy had given a cure-bottle to the messenger. She would provide fair warning of some dangerous spot to be looked out for on the road; then it rested with the carrier of the bottle to get past it safely, and usually with a time-limitation introduced for good measure.

It need not be concluded, of course, that Biddy was doing this to make her cures more precious, as it were. She may just as easily be seen as offering friendly advice about a mishap that would surely happen had she not given the warning. If the cure arrived safely and was administered according to her instructions all would be well. In certain cases, however, something more was necessary, such as the death of a valuable animal, to 'pay' for the cure. It is not clear whether this was to impress on the suppliant the seriousness of the favour granted or whether it was an offering to the Good People by Biddy in order to save herself from 'a gruelling'.

The cures and favours sought from Biddy were of three main types: (1) cures from sickness or disability; (2) cures for animals; (3) cures for 'infestation' or molestation by fairies.

Let us start positively and simply, where a cure was sought and granted, no more, no less:

'My mother used to tell a story about this lad that got the rabies an' he went kind o' mad out of it. An' they tied him in a horse-car and they brought him to Biddy an' she cured him. An' he went back sitting on the rider o' the car. He was fine.

'Now, I was in Shanagolden one time an' I bought turkeys from a woman there. I declare to God, I hadn't 'em bought a minute when I told her where I was from an' she said,

'"D'you know Feakle?"

'"I do o' course," says I.

'"What kind was Biddy Early," says she, "at all?"

'I told her, an' didn't she tell me about this man that went tied with a rope to Biddy in a horse an' car. Who was it but the very same man that my mother told me about! An' he came out o' that very yard in Shanagolden. Wasn't that a coincidence?'[71]

The following, in its very simplicity, is reminiscent of some of the Gospel accounts of cures worked by Christ:

'There was this woman from the country up, Kilanena side, came down to Biddy one time. Her daughter got paralysed, an' before that she was learning step-dances an' was good at 'em, too. Well, she came down, the mother, an' the daughter had a pair o' crutches. Now Biddy, she was married to Flannery at this time, an' Flannery was a fiddler. An' whatever medicine she gave to the little girl she took one crutch from her an' she put it on her knee an' broke it in two or three pieces an' threw it into the fire. An' the little girl began to scream an' bawl.

'"How," says she, "will I move about at all now?"

'"Ah," says Biddy, "you won't want it," doing the same with the other one. An' she told the husband to play a tune there, an' told the young girl get up an' dance her steps. Up she got an' danced steps as good as ever she did. Oh, that's a fact.'[72]

The very brevity of the next example, and the oddness of the ailment, invite further exploration, but no more information was forthcoming:

'. . . an' my brother-in-law, he told me that when he was a child he came in there, an' he saw a man in the bed with a cock's comb on him. They brought him to Biddy Early after that, an' she cured him. I know no more!'[73]

Sometimes she saw fit to put a penance on the person as a condition of the cure, as in this case:

'My father's stepfather was living here, an' below at the cross o' Tubber they used to pitch an' throw a stone that time. An' you heard tell o' forts, didn't you? Well, he went in cutting the fort in a neighbour's place, an' he got a thorn in his finger. O, very bad. Whoever the surgeon was in Ennis at the time, he told him that he'd have to lose the hand to stop the poison. An' he was old, an' "by the holy Janey," he says, "I won't do without my hand till I see Biddy Early."

'An' he went straight to Biddy's, where she lived, an' he was going up the street to her house – he never saw her before or neither did she see him. "O, Johnny," she says, "you'll keep away from the whitethorns an' forts in Tubber again."

'He knew he was right then. He said to himself he was going to be cured. So she cured him, an' told him go home. But she put a penance on him, that he could not stay at the cross o' Tubber for a certain time, but should pass it by. That wasn't so easy because he used to be ever with the boys pitching, sure, an' throwing stones. But faith, if he went, he had to take the penance with him, an' keep away from the cross. And she cured him.'[74]

In all the above cases the afflicted party came in person to Biddy and so got a direct answer, but in cases where the cure had to be taken home to a sick person or animal there, the safekeeping of the cure could be a formidable condition in itself. The following examples demonstrate this:

'There was a man o' the Neylons up here an' he was sick, an' his brother went down to her. An' she gave him a bottle o' something for him. But she told the lad to mind the bottle coming home for fear anything'd happen it. An' d'you know, there's a little stream o' water crossing the road below there, coming from the blessed well. But isn't it there the horse got frightened an' reared an' everything. But he minded the bottle.

'She knew they'd try to stop him bringing it all the way home. That's why she gave him the warning.'[75]

That the attempted interception should have occurred near a well is not entirely surprising (see chapter 3).

In this next account, ability to withstand prolonged fear rather than just one sharp encounter is the testing factor:

'There was another fellow that went down to Biddy. I forget now what he wanted to have done, but she told him, she said,

'"You'll meet a goat," she says, "on the road, an' he'll be rubbing himself up agin you. But don't hit him," she says. "If you do you'll never make the journey home."

'Lord God, he was coming below Drumcanora Bridge an' didn't the goat leap out over the road, started bawling at him, an' she frightened him. Well, that goat conveyed him up a good mile o' the road, an' whatever she met on the side o' the road, she used to rub up an' down with her horns. An' the lad never stopped, only prayed to God that he'd never live another night like it. He nearly died with the fear, you know.'[76]

There is just enough room for doubt here to keep us wondering: is the goat friendly or otherwise, protecting him, or daring him to hit it, thereby spoiling his mission?

The next example shows us that the enemy did not have to be frightening, or even unfamiliar. It could take the rather innocuous form of a neighbour anxious to have a friendly chat:

'This man – I knew him well – he got sick, an' he was very bad, so the father went down across to Feakle, walking. 'Twas a melting summer's day in the month o' June. She gave him the cure, whatever it was, but she says,

'"There's one thing I'm going to tell you. If you aren't at home before the sun'll set, that cure'll be no good."

'So he came, as fast as he could, an' he was very nearly home, about a mile across the land. Sure, he was very tired, but he met an oul' woman on the road. She happened to be living near there an' she came out talking to him. An' 'twas near a bridge – the river was running underneath. An' I declare to God, with the blathering he didn't feel the time going. He gave a look at the sun, an' Jays, half of it was gone there above behind the mountain. He got up, but he barely made it in time before the sun was gone. He administered the cure. The lad got better, but his head was always sideways. Every other way he was perfect, but the head was that way to the day he died. The delay that did it, an' they put that mark on him. If he was there five minutes sooner the head'd be straight.'[77]

There is little doubt in this speaker's mind as to who was responsible for the permanent injury to the man's neck. 'They' near the end says it all.

In other cases sheer tiredness, or complacency, proves to be the undoing of the cure:

'Another man, the Tailor Shannon, he went down to her when there was something wrong with a beast, an' she gave him a bottle an' she told him "Now, for the peril of your life," she said, "don't cross any land till you arrive at home. Keep on the road."

'An' she gave him this little bottle an' he put it in his pocket. But he was so tired after the long journey that when he was coming over here the top road, down by the castle, you know, he was too lazy or tired to go down six or seven hundred yards to come over the village, an' didn't he come down across a short cut from the top road, straight into his own house. He said to himself "devil a great harm" – he was tired. An' there's a fall o' ground down. But didn't he slip, an' fell, an' there was a stone under his hip an' he broke the bottle. An' she knew that was going to happen. So, she told him fact.'[78]

Here it is difficult to see why Biddy should have given the cure in the first place if she knew that the mishap was going to occur, as the speaker suggests. It would seem to boil down to a question of 'did it happen because she knew it?' or 'did she know it because it was about to happen?' *Post hoc* or *propter hoc*, who can tell?

Sometimes if the person did get home safely, there was one final obstacle: to administer the cure properly. Failure to do so guaranteed the loss of all that might have been gained up to then, as we see in the following:

'There was a girl there outside Kilkishen, a fine girl, an' she was done up. So they went to Biddy for her an' they brought the cure with 'em. An' she told 'em, at a certain hour o' the night to mind her; if they heard any noise, to mind her.

'The certain hour o' the night came, between one an' two o'clock. The whole yard began to fill up with horses, an' they leaping an' tearing an' jumping. They all ran out o' the house to see 'em. When they came in the girl was gone back into the same image as she was before the bottle came, an' they went to Biddy again.

'"Ah, says she, "ye let her off."

''Twasn't she was in it at all, Biddy made out, only an image. She died after a while.'[79]

It is easy, from this, to see why Biddy might receive rough treatment from the Good People, since she was helping to take a human victim from them.

Another example:

'At that time they say the Good People used to bring the women, married women. Now, this man, he got up one morning an' wasn't his wife an' child gone. But there was a big fort at the back o' the house, an' didn't he go to Biddy an' she told him that the wife an' the little child was athin in the fort. An' she gave him a bottle an' she said,

'"Stay outside now an' sit there until they're going out."

'An' when they were going out she told him to fire the bottle. An' he fired the bottle an' hit the little lad. An' he brought back the little child, but his wife was kept. An' I knew the little fellow that was brought back. He was an oul' man when I knew him. But he wasn't able to tell what was inside in the fort. He was too young.

'An' they said that the woman used to be seen in the fort. She had red hair, the Lord have mercy on her.'[80]

Probably the most detailed example of this type of story that I came across was told to me by the late Jimmy Armstrong of Ballyroughan, Quin:

'On the road below Kilkishen a man lived whose name was Gasty Mac. An' Gasty got sick, an' he was sick for about twelve or fourteen days, an' 'twas worse he was getting. An' for that whole time there were hundreds o' magpies above in the thatch o' the house an' they rooting it an' picking ribs out of it an' throwing 'em down.

'But when Gasty was getting no better his wife decided to go to Biddy Early. Biddy had then left Carrowroe an' married above in Kilbarron, near Feakle. But anyway, Gasty's wife got a man to drive her in a horse an' sidecar up to Kilbarron, which was about fifteen miles by road.

'When they arrived Biddy was standing at the door, an' without they ever opening their mouth or even mentioning anything she says to the man driving, "You drove Mrs Gasty Mac here to know would I cure her husband that's sick an' that was sick for the past two weeks. Well, Mrs Mac," says she, "I have bad news for you."

'"Are you Biddy Early?" says Mrs Mac to her.

'"I am Biddy Early, an' I have bad news for you, Mrs Mac. Now, since you left home your husband died. But he didn't die – remember that! An' in the past, while he was sick, there were hundreds o' magpies rooting the thatch out o' the house. But they weren't magpies at all. They were the fairies. An' 'twas they brought your husband with 'em. An' when they bring someone they leave something to resemble that person in his place. Now, you'll bring him back, Mrs Mac, if you do what I'll tell you. Go back," says she, "now to Tulla or Kilkishen an' get the wake goods for tonight, whatever you'll need. Also, tell all the people that your husband died today an' tell 'em be at the wake tonight. An' tomorrow, tell the undertaker to bring the coffin an' the hearse to your door," says she.

'"Now, there's one thing that I'm going to tell you an' which you must abide by. Let no relative whatsoever touch the coffin, not even yourself. Only get four o' the strongest men in the parish to bring in the coffin to your husband's bedside. Take off the cover off the coffin an' get four black-handled knives – the knives must have black handles – an' put one at each corner o' the coffin an' turn the handles out towards the corner an' the blades in. When that's done – remember, now, 'tisn't your husband that's in the bed at all but a thing that was left there by the fairies – leave that in on top o' the four black-handled knives an' put on the cover on the coffin an' screw it down in the usual way. Then let the four strongest men in the parish take it on their shoulders, bring it to the four cross-roads an' leave it down at the fair centre of the cross. Let them take off the cover off the coffin then an' there'll be nothing in it only a brush. An' your husband will be sitting at his own fire when you go back home. Let you be standing by the side o' the coffin when they take off the cover an' you'll see there'll be nothing in it only a brush."

'Mrs Mac thanked Biddy an' went home. They got the four black-handled knives an' put 'em one at each corner o' the coffin with the handles out. They took the corpse that was in the bed – what they thought was Gasty Mac – an' put him into the coffin. They put on the cover, screwed it down, an' the four strong men took it up an' brought it to the door. Outside the door they put it on their shoulders an' every step they were taking 'twas heavier the coffin was getting. They had, I s'pose, about four hundred yards to go with it to the cross an' when they were gone about two hundred yards there'd be a half ton weight in it. They were warping under it. An' 'twas about to fall off their shoulders when Mrs Mac – she was walking behind it – she ran an' she put her two hands up to it.

'Immediately all the weight lifted. It got as light as a cork. They brought it up to the cross, left it down at the centre of the road an' took off the cover as Biddy had told her. An' when they opened it up he was inside in it the very same as they put him into it, the thing that was in the bed. Only this time he was dead for sure.

'An' if she did what Biddy told her, not to touch the coffin, she'd have brought him back from the fairies an' he'd be sitting inside at his own fire when she went home. So that's my story, now.'

The Good People also play a strong part in this next example:

'Neighbours that was here one time, a man an' his wife, an' here's what happened. Just at the cross there outside he was coming in his horse an' car one day, an' there did a big whirlwind come an' the horse was capsized an' he was thrown out on the road. An' after that he wasn't right in the mind. He had to be in bed the whole time. So she went to Biddy Early, an' she hadn't to ask her what brought her. She knew. Now, did you ever hear tell of lady fingers? – you know, the big flower that grows on the ditches? She told her to pull that an' boil it out an' let it cool, an' give it to him to drink.

'"He'll fall asleep then," she said. "An' under no circumstances don't wake him up."

'But he was so long asleep she thought he was dead, an' didn't she waken him up. The cure was no good then, an' he never was cured after that. But he could tell things. Supposing there was a man dead three miles away he could tell you in the morning that that man was dead without ever hearing it. He never got out o' the bed again!

'She gave people her cure, an' anyone that followed her instructions, they were cured.'[81]

There seems to be an element of compensation here, as if the man were being paid for the loss of his cure by the acquisition of an extraordinary gift. Something similar seems to be at work in the following:

'This gentleman, his horse got sick an' Biddy cured her, but she said that they'd have to put the sickness on something lesser, some other animal. They wouldn't agree to that at all – they were gentry, o' course.

'"Put it on the groom," they said.

'The groom was the father o' nine childer, an' the poor man was down next morning. The wife spotted it an' she came to Biddy an' she said,

'"Why did you do it to me?" says she, "an' I with nine childer?"

'"Ah, don't mind that," says Biddy. "He'll be all right. That oul' horse'll die. But as I *did* put you to trouble, now, I'll give you a gift of your own for to cure your own family, but nothing else. Not outside your own house."

'Whether she did cure or not, I don't know.'[82]

This is the only example I have met with in which Biddy gives away part of her power to atone for wrong done. Indeed, this is the sole story I collected in which Biddy does something bad without an obvious reason. There is another version, however, which exonerates her from blame, even though there is no mention of compensatory power for the injured party:

'I only heard one story against her, an' that was from an old man that lived up here in a cottage. His father was a groom to a man that had an entire horse. But, the horse got sick and the man that owned the horse was very near Biddy. Now, his wife's father, he hadn't a great name as names go, but he went to Biddy about the horse. Biddy said she'd do all she could,

'"But, what'll I put it on?" she says.

'"Ah," he says, "put it on the groom."

'The horse got better, but the poor groom, he was in a cripple an' his mouth was turned back to his ear, an' his hands was crippled too. But he was there in the bed, an' his wife was great friends with a broker in Limerick o' the name o' Johnny Horgan – his job was to sell the butter in the firkins. She scrambled in to Johnny an' told her story, an' he came out to Biddy. An' Biddy done all she could for the poor man. She brought him middling, but the mouth was still turned. But he was able to carry on. Dhera, there was nine or ten children. That was the only yarn we ever heard that she done bad to someone. But they really don't blame Biddy. 'Twas the oul' lad's fault. They made out that Biddy could do nothing when he said it.'[83]

Here we get a glimpse, perhaps, of a more malignant side of the power Biddy consorted with, the side that has given such power a feared reputation down through the centuries. Though nothing more can be said of it in Biddy's case since other manifestations of it do not exist, it is interesting to note it, nonetheless.

Many other examples of cures involving animals remain in the memory of the people and they could be quoted at length, but I have chosen the following four because they seem to me fairly to cover the question. They are quite similar, yet also subtly different. The first is straightforward:

'Martin Fahy, he was a postman in Quin, an' he knew Biddy as well as Biddy knew herself. An' there was a field at the end of his neighbour's house in Quin – the field is there yet – an' 'twould be a sheer height of about eight feet. An' you can see a stone wall built up against it. But, outside the stone wall there was a whitethorn hedge, an' the whitethorn hedge was growing up on a level with the top field, the field at the back of it. Well, the people that owned the field used to keep it cut, the hedge, not to let it grow any higher, d'you see, than the field. But anyway, the woman o' the house, one day she was spreading clothes out on the hedge to dry an' whatever kind of a stumble she got didn't she fall out on the hedge. An' she fell down at the other side. But, a stump o' the whitethorn, it stuck in her knee an', bedad, when she went in her husband, Tom, was inside an' she asked him to know could he get it out, the stump o' the oul' whitethorn. An' he couldn't. Next day the leg was swelled. She couldn't walk on it an' she had to stay in bed. The next day 'twas worse an' the husband went down to Martin Fahy an' he asked Martin to know would he drive him up to Kilbarron to Biddy, that she could cure the leg.

'Martin said he would, an' the people that owned the field, they had a horse an' sidecar, an' Martin asked 'em for it to drive Tom up to Kilbarron. They gave it to him, o'course.

'When they arrived in Kilbarron, anyway, Tom went into Biddy's house an' Biddy was sitting at the fire.

'"Well, Tom," says she when he went in the door, "your woman was spreading clothes yesterday at the back o' the house on a hedge, an' she fell out on the hedge an' a stump o' the whitethorn stuck in her knee, an' you came up to me to know would I cure her. An' Tom," says she, "I *will* cure her. An' I have it here," says she, "made up an' all, a bottle that you must give her three spoonfuls of. An' you have a valuable greyhound, an' that dog," says she, "will pay for the cure. So take this bottle, an' when you go home, your greyhound will be lying in front o' the kitchen fire. Now, when you give your wife the first spoonful o' this bottle the greyhound," says she, "will disappear out an' come back in the morning. An' when you give her another spoonful o' the bottle the greyhound is gone again until the following morning. And when you give her the third spoonful of this bottle your greyhound will pay for the cure."

'He took the bottle, anyway, an' himself an' Martin Fahy, they drove back to Quin. Tom went in an' his wife was inside in the bed. He took the cork out o' the bottle an' gave her a spoonful of it. The dog was in front o' the fire an' he started barking an' off out the door with him in a run. The dog was seen no more that evening. 'Twas about ten or eleven next day when he came back.

'An' the next evening Tom gave her another spoonful o' the bottle. The dog started barking again in front o' the kitchen fire an' off he went again. Seen no more that evening or until about the same time next day. An' Biddy had Tom told not to give the spoonful o' the bottle to his wife until the dog came back the third time. An' when he came back Tom gave the third spoonful o' the bottle to his wife. The dog lay down in front o' the kitchen fireplace an' died. So that dog paid for that woman's cure. An' that's my story.'[84]

The following shows a price having to be paid and also advice being given for the future:

'There was a father an' son an' they lived in Slievanore. But, they were going to the fair o' Feakle with cattle, an' they came as far as

Corlea. An' coming up where the bridge is they met a woman there. They had the cattle out before 'em, an' this man, didn't he step in an' let her pass in the road. The next thing, he fell down. He was on the rampart an' she brushed agin him, an' he fell down in the road. They let back the cattle as quick as they could, anyway, an' they went to someone living there an' got a horse an' car to bring him on. An' they went down to Biddy Early's an' they told her. She said:

'"Why did you leave the road? Because if you held the road nothing'd happen to you. An' don't ever leave the road again," she said. "Well, go home now an' you'll be all right. But the best cow you have is a speckled cow, an' that cow'll be dead tomorrow morning," she said. "But don't tell anybody. Bury the cow."

'But that man had a lame step every day of his life after. He had.'[85]

The very same advice applied to anyone who met the *cóiste bodhar* (headless coach): never give way to it on the road. By doing so the advantage passed to 'Them' and anything might happen as a consequence. The problem, of course, lay in keeping one's nerve. How many people, taken unawares on a dark stretch of road by such an apparition, would remain calm enough to stand consciously against the rumble of approaching hooves and wheels? Very few, it can safely be said.

Near Tulla I was told the following story by a woman who preferred to remain anonymous:

'Some man that came to her had a very sick cow at home an' she made up this bottle of herbs, or whatever she made it up of, an' told him to dose the cow an' then bury the bottle when they'd be finished with it. The cow was lying down when he came but when he gave her the dose she jumped up an' was as right as the mail. An' a couple o' years went by, an' they had a child that was very, very sick, an' no doctor could do anything for her. The child was actually dying. An' he said,

'"Oh, great God, I'm going out an' digging up Biddy Early's bottle, an' we'll see."

'An' he gave a drop o' the bottle to the child an' the child jumped up an' was as right as ninepence. But when he went out another animal was dead outside. An' he came back to Biddy, an' she said,

'"Go 'way! Go 'way! You didn't do what you were told. I can't help you now."

'So she had just so much power.'

Perhaps the conclusion here should be that Biddy did not wish her cure to be used for any purpose other than the one she specified. She certainly appears agitated here, maybe because she understood more clearly than anyone else the dangers as well as the benefits of the power she was dealing with.

The man in the next case, which on the face of it, seems very much the same as the previous one, got off much more lightly. Maybe Biddy was in a better humour on the day:

'A man beyond near me had two horses, an' one of 'em got sick an' done up, so he had to go to Biddy. An' she gave him a bottle for the horse. He came back an' he gave half of it to the horse, an' the horse was up perfect next morning.

'A while after an oul' sow he had got done up, an' he gave her the rest o' the bottle. But didn't the horse get knocked out again. So he went back to Biddy and told her his story. She said,

'"You thought more of the sow than you did o' the horse."

'She told him what he done with the bottle an' you'd think she shouldn't know it at all. So she gave him another bottle for the horse, told him not to use it for anything else only the horse. An' the horse got all right. You see, what she gave you the bottle for, you had to use it for that an' nothing else.'[86]

It would certainly seem that there was just sufficient power in each cure given by Biddy to do the specific job for which it was intended, and that once the cure had been assigned to its goal it could not be changed without risk of injury.

We come now to that worst of all cases, where a crucial choice depended not on Biddy but on the suppliant. The father in the story about to be told by P. Murphy should have known where his duty lay, but under circumstances of stress, which of us can tell how we might behave?

'This man, he was married an' he had one child. An' his wife died. He married secondly. But he had a great horse an' 'twas that horse was going to make a living for him, because he used to till a bit, an' car, an' do everything. Without the horse he couldn't get on. But the horse got sick an' they didn't know what was wrong with her. An' there was no vets that time so they hit to Biddy, an' he told her his story.

'"Oh, I know all that," says she. She knew it all.

'"You have one child."

'"I have."

'"An' you're married again. Well, you're going to lose that child now, or either the horse. One of 'em is going to go. But whichever one you prefer to go," she said, "that child will sneeze tonight at twelve o'clock three times. If you want to save the child you'll say 'God bless us', an' if you don't, but want to save the horse instead, don't say anything. But if you say 'God bless us' you'll have the child, but you won't have the horse. So it's up to yourself," says she. "Yourself is the boss. Go home, an' God speed you."

'He came home anyway, an' he chatted it with his wife, the stepmother to the child.

'Anyway, it came on to the twelve o'clock. They sat by the fire, an' the stepmother commented that it wasn't right to let any human being go for an animal. But he said,

'"You know the position we're in."

'They were as poor as Job's cat, an' if the horse went they were hooked. That's what *he* thought. Well, they went to bed anyway, but there was no sleep when this big decision had to be given. The child sneezed at twelve o'clock, once. No word. Sneezed again. No word. He sneezed a third time, an' the stepmother said, 'God bless us.'

'"Why did you say it?" says he.

'"If his mother was here she'd say it," says she.

'They went out in the morning an' the four horse's legs were cocked. I consider her a great stepmother. There was breeding behind her. There was nature behind her, anyway. That was a big undertaking, an' the husband against it!

'An' they got on great after, built up until they were well off. But if he had his way that night, on through the rest o' their days they'd have a torture of a life.'[87]

While on the topic of favours sought from and granted by Biddy there is one rather odd case which may be mentioned here – a request for invisibility. Let Jimmy Armstrong tell us about it:

'There did this woman go to Biddy for some cure or something one time. An' there was a fair in Tulla at the time an' she had to go through the street o' Tulla, an' the street was all packed with cattle buying an' selling. But, 'twas an ass an' car she had. She went to Kilbarron, anyway, an' she told Biddy that she *hated* to go through the street o' Tulla, that there was a fair on there, an' she had messages to get when she was going back home. An' Biddy says to her,

'"Well, Mrs Murphy," says she, "I'll put you, now, in the way that the people in the fair won't trouble you, because," says she, "you won't see one person in Tulla when you're going back. Now, Mrs Murphy, come out here in the yard."

'She went over to the wall an' she got a small stone out of it.

'"Now, Mrs Murphy," says she, "put that into the pocket o' your coat an' when you're going in through the street o' Tulla there won't be one person there. An' when you go out o' the street o' Tulla," says Biddy to her, "you'll meet 'em going home, buyers an' sellers that didn't sell their cattle."

'She took the stone, anyway, that Biddy gave her an' she put it in her pocket. She got up on her ass an' car again, hit back from Kilbarron to Tulla, an' when she went into Tulla she couldn't see one person in the street. An' the people *were* there! That's sure.

'She went into the shops, a few shops, an' got her messages. She brought 'em out, sat up on her ass an' car again an' hit out o' Tulla. She wasn't gone, I s'pose, a quarter of a mile outside Tulla when she met the people bringing home their cattle from the fair.

'An' when she was going through Tulla there wasn't one there. Wasn't that strange?'[88]

Many questions might be asked about this particular case. Would Biddy really have acceded to such a trivial-seeming request? Why could the woman not have got her 'messages' in one of the nearby villages? If she had the leisure-time to go as far as Kilbarron, a distance of several miles, could she not have gone to Kilkishen and done her shopping there? If the woman's motivation for wishing to remain unseen is rather unbelievable here it is somewhat more convincing in this next version:

'This woman from Maghera, she had a cow that was very sick an' dying. O' course, there was no vets that time – there might be one in the whole county, an' the people couldn't afford vets anyway. An' someone told her to go to Biddy Early an' that she'd cure the cow. An' the following day there was a fair in Tulla, 25 March, one o' the noted fairs, an' she got up mighty early in the morning so she'd be gone through Tulla before the people'd be at the fair, because she was going barefoot. Whether 'tis the way she had no shoes now, or what, I don't know. But some o' the old people that time used prefer to go barefoot; they could walk better without any shoes. But she went anyway, barefoot, an' Biddy gave her this dose to give the cow, an' says she,

'"You'll have to have it given to her by such a time. But you'll make it. You're a good walker."

'"But," says the woman to her, "how will I pass through this fair o' Tulla going back, now? I have no shoes, an' won't they all be looking at me."

'Says she, "you'll see no one, nor there'll no one see you."

'An' she came down through the street o' Tulla. An' 'twas packed with cattle an' people, striking bargains an' everything, an' none of 'em saw Mrs Murphy, nor Mrs Murphy didn't see anyone.

'An' 'twas well known the time she passed that all the people an' all the cattle were there.

'An' the cow was up when she came home.'[89]

The animal, it seems, did not even need to be dosed. Perhaps the mere fact that the woman arrived home was enough!

Stories like this, howerver far-fetched they may appear, still strongly persist today. Only recently I collected a similar one about a priest who, not wishing to be seen drinking in a licensed premises by an officious parish priest, made himself invisible to his superior while remaining visible to all the other customers.

And if Biddy could grant invisibility to others, then more than likely she could take on that state herself. There is no story extant which would illustrate this, but many where she is seen to know what people did or said when the persons involved thought they were alone. The feeling that she was an all-seeing, eavesdropping, mysterious presence might help to account for the reluctance of many people, even today, to speak their innermost thoughts concerning her.

Having looked at cases where a favour was sought from Biddy, and granted, let us consider briefly some instances where she refused to help. As I have said previously, there were three basic reasons why she might refuse: if one had not sufficient faith in her; if she considered the ailment outside of her competence; if one had displeased her in some way.

Let us take the first of these.

'Another man that was above there in the mountain, he had blood-pressure, an' he was very bad with it. Some doctor that was in Sixmilebridge at the time, he leeched him. Anyway, when he was doing no good some o' the old people in the mountain went up to Biddy. Whatever token she had in the bottle she read it, an' she told 'em she could do no good for him, that they let the doctor bleed him.

Only for that she'd cure him, she said. Any place that a doctor went before her she didn't want to have no meddling in it.'[90]

Whether this antipathy to doctors was a personal thing or some condition laid on her is hard to tell. The information that remains is not specific on the matter. Yet when one considers the attitude of the learned professions today to those they would regard as amateurs doing their work, it is not to be wondered at that there might be mutual suspicion between the two sides in a time when religion, or the perceived lack of it, could colour attitudes as considerably as any question of professional competence.

Lack of faith in Biddy was one thing, but being too scrupulously religious could also have its dangers, as this example shows:

'My grandfather, I don't think he was much of a man for going to Mass or anything. But this neighbour of his was sick an' he wanted him to go to Biddy. He refused, because he was a sort of a holy man that was all one with the priests. But the grandfather kept at him, an' didn't he give in in the finish – he was getting worse – an' they struck down to Biddy. An' the grandfather saluted her. She looked at the lad that was sick. "You're coming to see me now," she said, "but you're late. You can go back. 'Tis all the same."

'An' he died a week after. She knew he refused to come in time. An' the same man was only about thirty years old at the time.'[91]

The impression one gets from Biddy's speech here is that once the man had not come to her early and of his own free will, there was nothing she could do for him, that choice, for her, did not enter into the case.

Somewhat similar is this next instance, though with the added dimension of a ghostly appearance:

'There was a woman about a half a mile from where we are now, an' she died. An' the priest that came to attend her an' she dying, he walked down the road, in the evening, a mild evening with the sun shining grand. An' a neighbouring man, he saw this woman, walking down the road after the priest. An' she leaned her hands in over the wall. An' that woman was dead above at home that time. The man that saw her, he thought she was only someone who wanted to talk to the priest or something. An' her husband an' a daughter was gone to Biddy Early at the time. Biddy said,

'"Sorry. Go home now. Your mother is dead. You didn't come in time," she said. An' at the very same time she was appearing near the priest. Wouldn't it put you thinking.'[92]

However, the following would appear to contradict the two previous examples, and seems to give Biddy much wider discretion. Could it be that honest scepticism was less odious to her than lukewarm faith?

'My grandfather went to Biddy one time. He was what they call softening cabbage, putting a butt of earth up to the cabbage-plants along in the haggard. An' someone was talking to him this day an' the conversation came down about Biddy. An' my grandfather began to laugh at the idea o' Biddy curing. He didn't believe at all, at all in Biddy, that she had any power or could cure anybody.

'But he was in the bog some time after, putting out turf. An' the fairy breeze passed. An' he threw a *caorán* at it, took up a *caorán* o' turf an' threw it. Straight away he got sick, an' he wasn't able to come home. He had to be brought home in an ass an' car, an' put into bed. An' he wasn't doing any good, or able to say anything, so someone said to him, "wouldn't you go to Biddy Early?"

'He had no faith in Biddy, but they persuaded him eventually, anyway, telling him how she cured this fellow an' that one. But wasn't he brought down to her in an ass an' car. An' she lived, it seems, some few yards in from the road, an' when they turned the ass in towards the house, she came up to the door an' she says,

'"Ha, Jimmy," says she, "are you coming to Biddy? An' all the laughing an' sneering you had the day you was softening the cabbage."

'But she cured him. Whatever she gave him she cured him.'[93]

In cases where the ailment brought to her door was not caused by the Good People Biddy seemed to be on less secure ground, and even though she might offer the benefit of her no-doubt-considerable medicinal skills she would not undertake to guarantee results, as the following shows:

''Twould be about 1859, around that time. An' the fever used break out in those days – whether 'twas typhoid or typhus, one or th' other, I don't know. But times were tough an' bad, an' the bits o' farms here an' there weren't much good.

'But anyway, my grandfather's brother an' sister both were sick an' he went along to Biddy. An' Biddy looked in the bottle.

'"Well," she said, "what's matter with your brother an' sister has nothing to do with what I do be dealing with. 'Tis a natural complaint, but a bad one."

'She told him not to give 'em hardly any food for a while, except drinks. An' she said,

'"Your sister, she'll be all right, but I'm afraid o' my life I can't guarantee the boy.."

'An' he died, an' she survived. An' Biddy never laid eyes on either one o' those, yet how well she knew!'[94]

The other reason why Biddy might refuse a cure, or cancel a cure already granted – displeasure – is at least eminently understandable. Most people's natural tendency would be to react in the same way. Take the following, for example:

'This man went to Biddy one time – a small little man down from the mountain – looking for a cure for someone at home, his wife or his mother. Biddy gave him the cure for her, a small little bottle, an' he put it in his pocket. An' she had a scissors there on the table, an' didn't he put the scissors in his pocket too an' went away with it. An' after a start she missed the scissors.

'"Bad luck to me, Johnny," she says, "but I'll bring you back again."

'He had to come again the next day, because she broke the bottle on the road.'[95]

It is difficult to understand how anyone could be so ungrateful as to steal from the person who was in the act of helping him. Maybe he did it to test her power – though one would have thought this unnecessary if he believed enough in her to come for a cure in the first place. How he was received when he returned can only be speculated on. It might seem that Biddy was acting in a somewhat underhand way here, playing a cat-and-mouse game with an unsuspecting victim, but the strange truth of the matter seems to have been that in cases where her own property was concerned she was as subject to the same limitations as the rest of mankind. If it were otherwise she would surely have faced him with the theft of her scissors before he left. (For other examples of this 'blind spot' see pp. 84-86.)

From all of the foregoing it can be seen that hundreds, if not thousands, came to ask favours of Biddy during her long residence at Kilbarron. It may be safely assumed that few came empty-handed. Seekers of favours rarely do. What then happened to Biddy's wealth? Or, more basically, what form did the offerings take? In chapter 2 we have seen that when Biddy got her bottle she was warned never to take any money for a cure or that her power would vanish. Most of those I spoke to agreed with this and maintained firmly that she accepted all kinds of groceries and much poteen and whiskey, but

never any money. However, a substantial minority of reliable informants expressed the conviction that she did in fact charge a fee, and
that this fee was one shilling. Let them speak for themselves:

'She had ·to get a shilling, you see, for this bottle. Other people
say she hadn't, you know, that there was no money involved, only
whiskey an' other things. But even though she used to get the bottles
o' whiskey too, there was no other payment but to give her the
shilling. That's all the payment. She had to get the shilling. I heard
my father saying that.'[96]

Perhaps there is an element of 'cross my palm with silver' here.
Whatever be the case, there appears to be a definite distinction
between payment (money) and gifts (whiskey etc.). It seems, though,
that Biddy had no fixed scale of charges. She allowed the good sense
and the means of the caller to dictate what the offering should be:

'She'd take a bob an' that was the outside of it. But what you
could bring her was a *taoscán* o' whiskey, a loaf or two o' bread, a
sweet cake, a bit o' bacon – something like that could be used. An'
she'd use every single bit o' that for the next visitor that'd come
along. She'd have nothing for herself, only for the next visitors.'[97]

This also answers for us the question of her presumed fortune. In
fact, as we shall see in chapter 8, far from amassing even moderate
wealth she died poor and had to depend on a charitable neighbour
for a decent burial.

But all that was far away, in years, if not from her mind, as she
plied her trade, dispensed her cures, during her heyday in Kilbarron.
Many and many a hopeful person ventured forth from that little
cottage clutching the precious bottle-cure, went home, administered
the cure and probably forgot about the bottle. It is with these bottles
that I wish to end this chapter.

How many of them were destroyed? Very few, one would imagine.
More than likely they were discarded, pushed into a hole in the wall,
or even buried. There must still be many of them hidden out there,
awaiting a lucky (or unlucky!) finder. The last word, on one such
bottle, I leave to Thomas Hannon:

'Part of our house in Réidh na hIománá was slated an' we were
rising the rest of it, so I went knocking the room, to do the job. An'
I came on this jar in it. 'Twas a pottery jar with a cork in it an' it
was about three quarters full o' stuff. So I went examining it.

'"Ah," says my father, "that's Biddy Early's bottle."

'An' my two brother's were young lads, about seven or eight years, an'

'"Go out an' bury that somewhere," he said to 'em.

'But I took the cork of it an' spilled it to see what sort the stuff was.

'"Cork that again! Don't mind that!" he said.

''Twas some rub the grandfather got from Biddy. 'Twas like water, but sort o' darkish. 'Twasn't clear at all.

'They went out with a spade an' hid the bottle somewhere. I took no notice. I was working away an' thought no more about it. But years afterwards, when the lads were grown men, I asked 'em did they remember the place where they buried it. They did o' course, they said, an' they'd find it. Well, they tried but they couldn't. An' they *wouldn't* get it whether they remembered where 'twas or not.'[98]

A mere failure of memory? Or something else? His final comment suggests that forces other than the dulling effect of time were at work.

Perhaps the Good People *do* look after their own property.

6: Telling and Foretelling

After the cures, no attribute of Biddy's made a greater impression on people's minds than the uncanny and unnerving way she had of greeting perfect strangers with intimate details of their lives and business that she could not possibly have known, but did. In many cases this knowledge was harmless, merely a matter of describing, for example, what the interior of a person's house looked like, but sometimes she could confront a caller with harsh or careless words he might have spoken of her at a great distance from her house, and this must have been a frightening experience. Everyone has something that might better remain hidden, 'and if she knows this about me, what else does she know?' Thus would the reasoning run. But at least such bluntness on her part could have one positive effect: it would encourage the truth, since what was the point of lying to such a one?

Whatever the niceties of people's reactions to Biddy's knowledge, it seemed in no way to hinder the flow of people to her door. Very likely it had the opposite effect. Curiosity is often stronger than fear; that and people's fascination with knowing what the future might hold would have assured her attractiveness.

It is hard for us, who have grown up with almost-instant communication, to understand how slowly news might travel in previous ages. It would probably be true to say that in the nineteenth century people in general did not know what was happening from day to day outside their own parish. Information spread at walking pace, so some of the startling facts that Biddy uttered would have made a far greater impression then than they might now. Who, in that age, could ever have foreseen a day when a mere child, by pressing a few digits on a little box, might make contact with America or even Australia? The very thought would have been laughed to scorn. But it has happened and has now become part of everyday life. If Biddy had done no more that this we might look on her today, with something less than awe, as a person with some kind of sixth sense, no more. However, she did much more than this. She foretold events which were many years in the future, and her prophecies were usually fulfilled in distressingly accurate detail. It is this aspect of her mystery that has not aged. Of course, it would be a foolish person who would say categorically that mankind will never manage to break the bonds of time and space, but until it happens Biddy will provoke a fascinated attention.

To reflect on the difference in the types of vision she was capable of I have divided the examples I use in this chapter into two broad categories, (a) Telling and (b) Foretelling. The distinction is in some ways an artificial one, yet it is useful for purposes of classification and it also serves to highlight another small category which cannot be ignored – happenings which she could not see or foresee. Just as, in the case of the bottle, Biddy did not seem in general free to accept money, so also here there appeared to be some prohibition on her from seeing beyond the present time and place when her own interests were concerned. Some of the blatant rogueries practised on her suggest that this blind spot was public knowledge. What seems remarkable, however, is that anyone would risk being found out when it was obvious that the retaliation that Biddy was capable of would be likely to be unpleasant indeed. Yet such deeds were done, and by neighbours, too, as we shall see.

Finally before getting to the examples themselves, it may be said that I could have put many of them in the previous chapter. For example, in the stories which I use here of butter being 'carried' through *piseógs* the people who went to Biddy obviously did go for a cure to their troubles, but much more pronounced in these cases, it seemed to me, was the desire to *know* who had done the deed. That Biddy could tell if she chose. I have had to judge each story on its merits and I hope that some readers at least will agree that I have chosen correctly.

We might do worse than start with a straightforward instance of Biddy telling a father of an injured son's whereabouts, thereby putting his mind at rest:

'They had a black horse up at Mick Sammon's place an' he went to give a run to this horse – I suppose he was stable-fed – an' he went down past here. But when he was coming back didn't the horse knock him coming up from Poll a' Trumpa an' landed at home without him. The oul' man, the father, caught the horse, jumped up on the saddle an' straight for Biddy Early. He landed below at her an' she said,

'"You're coming, an' you didn't come a minute too soon. Go home," she said. "He'll be all right."

'An' she told him exactly the place where he was knocked. She did. The oul' man, he didn't go down to where the son was, or anything, only home quick like Biddy said.'[99]

The father must surely have faced a dilemma. He would naturally have wished to rush to his injured son first, but to do so would have betrayed lack of confidence in Biddy and perhaps endangered a happy outcome. So suppressing his inclinations he obeys Biddy's order and goes home.

Some of the more readily recognisable features of the cure-tales (for example, the obstacle on the way home) appear in the next item, but there is also Biddy's explanation of apparently random misfortune as the workings of the Evil Eye, and the easing of the mind as well as the body of the sufferer.

'My grandfather, he was a great man for walking. He had a very lively step. An' he'd have to be waiting for 'em coming up from Mass; they'd be going slower an' he'd have to go a bit, an' stand till they'd get up to him. But he was coming this morning, an' a man from Inchamore was coming along with a horse and saddle, going home from Mass. An' just a few minutes before that some one o' the women said,

'"Johnny, you're an awful walker. Lord save us, but you're a fierce walker."

'A few minutes after, your man came along with the horse an' saddle, an' a paper blew off the road an' the horse shied an' went a bit sideways an' hit him over the ankle an' broke his leg. Ah, he suffered torture. Torture! He went to the bonesetter, an' the bonesetter fixed the leg. An' what in hell did he put into it but coarse salt, an' sure, it drove it stone mad, an' it all broke out around it. He went to some other one an' 'twas broken the second time, an' mended again. But 'twas going from bad to worse. So he went finally to the hospital in the old County Home in Loughrea an' he was there for a long time. But he came out, an' 'twasn't still right. So he said he'd go himself out to Biddy on horseback. An' he did, and she told him,

'"You was overlooked," she says, "on your way coming home from Mass. A certain woman said that you were a powerful great walker, the best walker she ever saw. The next thing, a horse passing by shied an' hit you with her shoe an' broke your leg."

'But she said,

'"I'll remove away all the pain, an' you'll be all right. You might be a bit lame, but that's not so bad."

'He used to have fierce pain in it up to this, you see.

'"Now," she said, "you're going home. Make sure you're inside in your own yard before the sun goes down."

'"Right," he said. "I think I ought to make it."

'"Well, now," she said, "you'd want to keep going fairly lively."

'So he came along, an' he took a short cut where they call it Bun a' Ghlas, an' as he looked over, the sun was going down. He could see the rim of it. An' from that moment onward, the sweat began to peel off o' the horse. An' big blobs o' froth as well as the sweat ran down fair on the road. But he got her into the yard with great scraping an' he put her in the stable an' did mighty rubbing on her – she was shivering. He was thinking he had a desperate load on her, whatever it was, but he could see nothing, only himself an' the horse.

'But that's what Biddy told him. And something strange was in that.

'The horse was all right too. An' the pain left the leg. But it was always a bit short.'[100]

This man was at least lucky to be rid of his pain. In the next tale Biddy, for whatever reason, does not lessen the suffering, only hints darkly at what may have caused it. This being poor consolation, the man goes off to gain relief where he may:

'My grandfather was watching a cow to calf in the month o' May an' 'twas a beautiful night. He heard two shots in the distance but he took no notice. An' next day he got an awful pain in his hand. Dreadful pain! But he went to Biddy an' she looked through her blue bottle, told him how he was doing his own business, an' the two shots he heard.

'"An' them weren't for your good," she said.

'But, very good. The pain didn't lessen. He couldn't get a wink o' sleep so he went in to Dr Moloney. But he wasn't at home, so he went up the priest, he was a Fr Donovan, to have a Mass offered. An' he told him how he went to Biddy an' what she told him. The priest got raging.

'"An' you went to the Devil," he said.

'"Well, Father," says he, "I'd go half road to hell if I thought 'twould ease the pain for me."

'So the priest calmed down an' took a cross from his inside pocket an' left it in the palm of his hand.

'"Go home," he said, "now, an' you'll sleep tonight."

'So he gave some money to the priest to have a Mass said, an' the pain left. But that hand was a lot thinner than the other after.'[101]

This is the only example I managed to find in which a sufferer is relieved by someone else after Biddy apparently fails to do so. It is a curiously inconclusive story in that Biddy neither cures nor offers an explanation for not doing so.

Much more decisive is her advice in the following:

'This man an' his wife, they were in bed one night an' this awful racket started outside, something like a party'd be fighting. An' it came on the roof o' the house. The man said he'd go out to see what 'twas about, an' clear 'em off. But the wife wouldn't allow him. So, the man got awful sick after that an' the wife went to Biddy Early. He was outrageous sick, now. An' Biddy told her about the terrible racket.

'"Well, if he went out he was finished. But he'll recover."

'An' so he did. The Good People that was in it. Biddy knew that.'[102]

The implication here is that the man insulted the Good People by the mere intention of going out to 'clear 'em off'. It took Biddy's knowledge to put his mind at rest and thereby hasten his recovery.

One of the areas where people would have sorely needed advice was in cases of *piseógs*, instances of evilmindedness in which persons unknown tried to steal the good luck of others through infernal means. As has been previously mentioned, most farmers' wealth lay in their dairy produce so not surprisingly this was the target of those whose purposes were evil. But it might be argued that the most serious effects of *piseóg*-working lay not in the specific losses to this or that farmer but in the suspicion sowed among neighbours, which in some cases could turn into generations-long feuds. Well within living memory such doings brought people to the courts of law, a particularly notable case being reported in Clare in 1958.[103] Because of this potential for ill effects it was extremely important to know the true culprit. But how could this be achieved, since the essence of *piseógs* is the secrecy attached to the working of them? Short of watching every field every day and night only luck or intelligent guesswork might bring a conclusion – unless, of course, there was someone who could tell when and where the deed might be done. Biddy, with her known skills of telling and foretelling and her knowledge of 'Them', was a natural source of advice and comfort. To illustrate this I have chosen three stories out of the many I have heard. The first shows that the discovery of the *piseóg*-worker could almost be as painful for the victim as for the culprit:

'Sure, my grandfather went over to her. He lived over there in Lisheen an' he couldn't make butter, an' someone advised him to go to Biddy, that she'd tell him. So himself an' a neighbour went over in a horse an' car – I often heard him saying it – an' 'twas three o' clock in the morning when they landed there, going from post to pillar. They knocked an' she opened the door, an she looked at him an' she said,

'"Welcome, John Casey, all the way from Lisheen where the moonlighters came from."

'"An'," he said, " you know me?"

'"I do," she says. "Come in, an' tell me what's wrong."

'He told her that he had six cows an' he was able to make butter, he said, every week, an' for the last month or that way the cream used rise up, making froth in the churn.

'"An' someone told me," says he, "to come here to you."

'"Well, John," says she, "as you came all the way now from Lisheen, d'you know what you'll do, an' you'll find out for yourself what's wrong?"

'An' he said he'd do whatever she'd tell him.

'"Have you a small field?" she said.

'"Ah, wisha, I have," he said. "There isn't any of 'em very big, no more than a couple of acres.'

'"Well," says she, "is there a hedge in 'em? Go into a small field where there's a hedge. An' put your top-coat on you," she said, "an' put another one down on your head, an' cover yourself up as good as you can. An' lie down under the hedge an' leave the cows in the field for the night. An' if she don't come one night she'll come the next."

'So he did. An' the first night, oh he said 'twas pure cod. But the next night he said he'd chance it again. An' don't you know, cows long ago, 'twas easy frighten 'em. But didn't they run, an' he looked an' saw the woman. An' when she came into the field she had a bucket an' he knew her straight away. But he said nothing, only came out from under the hedge. She began to roll down across the field, an' the cows went mad. An' she stood up an' she looked at him, an' he said,

'"I thought you'd be the last one to do it."

'"Twas one of his own neighbours that was doing it. An' the churn was right after.'[104]

This piece also shows us, by the way, how patient a person Biddy must have been, to greet a visitor with courtesy at 3 a.m.

Though most of those who brought their butter-problems to her were satisfied, there were a few who were not, as we find in this story:

'I heard tell of people who went to Biddy from Crusheen. They were two widow women an' they had two cows each. An' one of 'em had only a poor thin hungry-looking cow as well as a good one, but the other one had two great cows. But the woman with the bad cow had twice as much butter as her, an' she couldn't know how 'twas done. An' they used be arguing an' fighting. But the woman with the good cows went to Biddy.

'"Dhera," she says, "go home out o' that. 'Tis the' oul' cow ye have that ye do be rising on the wall when she'll fall, that's the cow that has it all."

'Well, she came home, an' from that day until the day they died they were fighting.'[105]

From this it would appear that although Biddy might point out a solution to a problem, the application of her advice rested with people themselves.

The same truth (i.e. that one must help oneself before being helped) applies to the couple in the next example, in a way we have already met with in the previous chapter:

'Here where we're living now, there was eight cows, an' th' oul' man an' woman, they'd be my great-grandfather an' - grandmother. An' he was going down to Biddy drinking the whiskey at night, going on *cuaird*.

'But the old woman wasn't able to make the churn. She could stay twisting nearly for the day an' 'twould only turn into oul' oil. So he proposed that she should go down to Biddy.

'"Not at all," she says. She wouldn't go near her. "'Tis enough to have you going in it."

'But she tried the churn for another two or three turns, an' finally she took her shawl an' put it down on her head, an' she went down to Biddy.

'"O! You're welcome," Biddy said. "Why didn't you come when your husband asked you? Only for the decent man I'd do nothing for you," she said.

'So poor woman couldn't say much.

'"Go home," she said, "an' put your cream in the churn in the night, an' get up in the morning before the sun'll rise an' you'll be able to make the churn."

'She came home an' did as she was told an' she hadn't four or five twists given to it until she had a lump o' butter.'[106]

More important than the cure here is the knowledge Biddy had of the woman's unwillingness to come to her of her own free will. However, one might say that Biddy, or anyone else who was observant, could guess reasonably accurately from the general demeanour of a visitor what that person's attitude was. What is not so easy to account for is the large number of instances in which she goes much farther, and actually tells people what they said in their own homes or on their journey prior to visiting her. Take the following:

'There was two brothers over here an' one of 'em had a cow sick. They had the vet, an' there was nothing could be done for her. An' John said to Pat,

'"What about we going to Biddy Early?"

'"Dhera," says Pat, "that oul' bitch, she'd do you more harm than good.'

'"We'll go anyway," says John.

'Off they went with Pat's horse an' car – 'twas John's cow was done up – an' they landed beyond at Biddy.

'"By God," she said, "you have great faith in me, John. But sure Pat said I was an oul' bitch. But," she said, "that's all right. Ye'll go home, but before ye'll be at home your horse'll be dead. He's dying now. But this man's cow," she said, "she'll be all right tomorrow."

'And so they were. But how right she was able to tell it!'[107]

Biddy's attitude might seem to smack of vindictiveness, but the teller insists that it was Pat, by his attitude, that condemned the horse to death, not Biddy. This desire to exonerate Biddy from all blame in a doubtful situation has already been noted (p. 57).

Less serious in its consequences, but just as startling to the person 'overheard', is the case described in the following:

'A house where we used to go on *cuaird* when we were young, I often heard the man o' the house telling it, that himself an' two other men walked it up to Biddy. An' he going up the boot was hurting him an' his foot got sore, so he said,

'"The Devil fire you, Biddy."

'But the minute he landed 'twas the first thing she hopped to him –

'"You're coming to me now," she said, "for a cure. An' you were cursing me on the way up."

'I heard him telling that, now, several times.'[108]

Maybe it was because there clearly was no malice behind his remark that she took the matter no farther.

In the next example, the narrator, Johnny Broderick, is obviously far more interested in the fact that Biddy could tell what people were saying about her many miles away than in the object of the visit – obtaining a cure from the effects of the Evil Eye:

'There was a man down there, he was six foot two in his socks, an' built accordingly. A fine man. But something happened him – maybe his nerves gave up or something. But, he went out to Biddy, an' as big a man as he was, he had a very small little wife – she was only between four an' five feet high. An' he was a very decent man.

'"*Tanam 'on diabhal*," he said, " I'd want to bring out a couple of bottlíns o' whiskey to poor Biddy."

'"Dhera," says his wife, "isn't one little bottle enough for that oul' damn hag."

'But he went out to Biddy, anyway. She welcomed him.

'"You're welcome," she said. "A decent man. You're a lot decenter than your little *smearachán*[109] of a wife."

'She could tell what they said in their own house before ever they set off! She looked at him.

'"You got a new waistcoat," she said. "An' the man that said 'You're a damn fine man now with that new waistcoat', he's the one that started your trouble."

'"Twas the man that praised the waistcoat that overlooked him, you see. But whatever she done with him, he was the finest again.'[110]

If critical, slighting words were apt to anger Biddy, so also was levity when a more serious attitude was called for, as we see here:

'All them women in Slievanore, they was a pure fright, you know. They came from the north of Ireland, you see, an' they had a cure nearly for everything. They was different to the natives.

'But this man, he was working with Burkes o' the big house at Marblehill, an' his wife got done up. An' when he came in, they said to him that he'd have to go to Biddy in the morning. An' he said,

'"I'll tell you what I'll do. I'll go to Biddy Early an' I'll stop with her."

'So finally he struck out in the morning for Biddy. 'Twas a long road from Ballinakill to Feakle an' Kilbarron. He went in, anyway.

'"Welcome, Jack," she said. "You're coming to stop with me?"

'Shook him to the ground!

'"Didn't you say last night that you were coming to stop with me?"

'"Ah, God, I can't," he said.

'"Well, go home," she said, " an' she'll be all right. But only for you having Biddy Earlys at home," she said, "you had no business coming to me."

'There was smart people at home, you see, that knew about the fairies. Oh, the people from the north, they knew all them things.'[111]

Was it to teach the man to have regard for his wife's condition that Biddy pulled him up so sharply, or to show him that in coming to her he was engaged in no frivolous mission? Whatever the reason, he no doubt had food for thought on his journey home.

The journey of the girl described next was also eventful and demonstrates that not alone could Biddy hear people at a distance; she could also, apparently, see what they were doing:

'There was a publican in Tulla by the name of O'Brien. But he had a girl working with him an' he sent her to Biddy with two or three bottles o' whiskey. But the girl was great with some man that was fond o' whiskey an' when she was going over the road she hid it in a furze bush, one bottle – thought Biddy wouldn't miss it. She went over then an' delivered her message. Biddy took it an' she says to her,

'"You can thank Mr O'Brien from me," she says, "for the whiskey, but go back now an' go to the furze bush an' bring me th' other one."

'She knew.'[112]

Note that Biddy does not punish the girl. But neither does she allow herself to be cheated. This story, though, is in contrast to others which show us Biddy as being unable to help herself when her own personal affairs were in question (see p. 85).

However much allowance might be made for a young girl, moreover a girl in love, precious little time had Biddy for those who ought to have had more sense but who yet persisted in their foolishness:

'There did two lads go fooling her one time. They went, an' one of 'em said he had a pain in his leg or something. She looked at him.

'"You have no pain in your leg," she said. "There's nothing wrong with you. But you aren't gone home yet," she says.

'An' they had a pony an' trap, an' the pony ran with 'em going home an' he broke his leg.'[113]

What a pity that a sensible animal should have to pay for the stupidity of its 'master'.

But that Biddy had a clear sense of justice is shown in this piece:

'Three Tulla men were out hunting, you know – an' all those people that'd go to her for a cure, they'd bring loaves o' bread, tea an' sugar, an bottles o' whiskey. An' she had a shed an' the stuff used be up to the roof, nearly, in the shed. But those three Tulla men went in, an' one of 'em was a very decent man; he wouldn't do any mischief.

'But she had an old woman that used to keep company with her, an' the old woman was sitting down in the corner. An' she let down plenty bread an' tea an' gave 'em whiskey too. So, when the fellows that weren't good-mannered started breaking up the bread an' pelting it at th' oul' woman that was sitting down in the corner, she said,

'"Well, ye can be going now, but maybe ye *wouldn't* go."

'So, it was duskish, you know, an' they walked away out. Well, they were going through hedges an' ditches all night until they were torn to pieces. But he never got a scratch, the man that did nothing. That's a fact. That happened.'[114]

Finally, before turning to Biddy's foretelling of future events, let us consider for a moment a short tale told to me in Peterswell, near Gort, in which the usual roles are somewhat changed. Here, the visitor is telling Biddy what *he* saw. But he is quickly silenced by her ominous reply:

'In that time there wasn't much clocks in the country an' this man, he got up to go to the fair o' Loughrea. An' he went into the fair, but he was too early an' there was no one in it. But didn't he see Biddy coming out o' Morrissey's yard an' she riding on a white horse. He knew her 'cos he was up to her a few times before that for cures.

'Anyway, a while after he went up again with a woman that something happened, an' he had a jennet an' car, an' he brought the woman up. An' Biddy called him by his name. An' he said,

'"I saw you one morning very early coming out o' Morrissey's yard riding on a white horse."

'"Ah," she said, " you do see too much. Don't be talking o' my name any more," she says. "You mightn't be the better for it."

'That was the last anyone heard of it from him.'

The man obviously believes Biddy to be 'in the fairies', an impression that she strengthens by her reaction to his news.

I have heard several versions of this story, without Biddy, and in every case the person on the horse is either one of the Good People or a human being 'in the fairies' voluntarily or as a result of being 'carried'.

That telling and foretelling merge imperceptibly into one another is, I think, shown by the next several stories. The first of these is the sole example in Irish in this collection, and it displays one startling difference from all the others, i.e. the insulting language used to Biddy by the suppliant. It may be excused on the grounds that he is not quite sober, and perhaps this is why Biddy takes no notice of it, yet it suggests that in the Irish-speaking tradition language of a more robust nature was accepted. This may also apply to behaviour since in no other story except this one have I found any mention of Biddy kissing or being kissed by a visitor.

'This man, he borrowed a neighbour's horse, drawing turf with her. An' she had lost a shoe an' got a bit lame, so he left her there. But, I own to God, didn't she follow another horse that was passing the road, an' went off. Some man got her miles away. He tended to her shoe an' put her in with his own horses when he saw no one coming to claim her. An' when no one came he said he'd use her. He had a lot o' ploughing to be done, you know.

'The man that owned her, anyway, when there was no trace of her, he went to Biddy Early. He came in the street. Biddy knew well what he wanted. An' she put her two hands around him.

'"Muise, Seán," adúirt sí, "cé bhfuil atáir?" – Seán McCarthy was his name.

'"Muise, cé bhfuil atáir féin?" adúirt sé, agus bhain sé póg di. "Agus beidh mé níos fearr amárach t'réis dul isteach faoi do lochtaí bocht. Is mise buachaill maith den rath," adúirt sé – you know, that "I'm a good boy for the women."

'But anyway, she took him in, an' she had whiskey, an' they drank, the two of 'em. An' he got drunk. An' when he was going home an' she was putting him in the car, she had nothing said about his horse when he said,

'"Ó, tanam 'on diabhal, a stríopach bhradach, níor dúirt tú fós liom cá bhfuil mo láirín."

'He was drunk this time, you see, softening out.

'"Ná bí imní ort. Inseoidh mé dhuit. Beidh sí agat i lá amháin," says the oul' lady to him.

'"Téir abhaile," adúirt sí, "agus imigh ar maidin agus geobhaidh tú do chapaillín. Téir chomh fada leis an farraige ó thuaidh agus *geobhaidh tú í agus í ag treabhadh le capall eile."*

'An he *did* go, himself an' another man – a horse an' car they had – an' didn't he see her within the garden ploughing at another man.

'Nuair a chonaic sé ag treabhadh í istigh ins an gharraí níor stop sé aon áit ag dul thar an balla, ach ag téaráil isteach tríd an balla, briars an' whitethorn an' all. An' the man, when he saw the devil coming, he made off an' he had the luck o' the Lord, because he'd kill him. He'd pull him out o' one another.

'Dá mbeadh mo lámhaí leagtha ort mharóinn thú chomh siúrálta leis an lá inniu ann,' adúirt sé.[115]

Note that Biddy here partakes of the whiskey with her guest, whereas in another account I was told quite vehemently that she was a non-drinker:

'An' her house was full o' whiskey. But she never drank.'[116]

In the next example, also concerning an animal, we see Biddy correctly foretelling a future outcome:

'My own father this happened to. He had a heifer, a fine beast, an' one morning he went out an' got the heifer gone out o' the field near the house. He thought nothing o' that. 'Twasn't the first time she went on the road. He searched for her, anyway, but high up or low down he couldn't find her. So he went to Biddy an' she looked through her bottle an' told him where his heifer was.

'"But you'll never get her," says she. "You'll see her from you, but you'll never again own her."

'Well, that was strange kind o' news, but he said he wouldn't let it stop there, so he asked her where he'd find the heifer.

'"Go over to Scariff," says she, an' she named a butcher there. "You'll find your heifer with him, but remember what I told you."

'He went off, an when he came to the butcher's yard he looked in an' there she was inside – he knew her well. He went in to the shop, demanded his animal. But the butcher told him,

'"I bought her at the fair here in Scariff. I paid good money for her." They argued it out, but he was getting no satisfaction. So he went for the police – the old RIC that was there that time. There was nothing they could do for my man. The cow was bought legal, so he had to come home without her. An' that was the way Biddy told him 'twas going to be.'[117]

The loss of such a beast could have been a serious blow to the man, and must in the circumstances have been annoying, but it was as nothing compared to the outcome of the following:

'Did you hear about the man that had the three cattle gone an' they were gone for three months?

'They were two brothers, they had a farm between 'em, an' they weren't pulling very happy with one another, d'you know. But these three cattle belonging to one o' the brothers were gone, anyway, an' he had the country searched for 'em. They broke out, I s'pose, an' strayed away. He notified the peelers, but no trace of 'em. He was in an awful way, o' course, so his neighbours told him,

'"You'll have to go to Biddy Early."

'That's what he did, an' he told Biddy his story – that the cattle were three months gone; they went in the springtime an' 'twas summer now. He told her that he had a brother at home with a two-acre field where he used to put in the cows for the length they'd be milking, but now, when the cows were missing, he was growing hay in the field.

'She looked in the bottle an' she said to him,

'"Was there a white one amongst 'em?"

'"There was, then," he says.

'"I know where they are all right," she says. "They're two miles south o' Tulla' – telling him the road they were in an' the place. Dhera, land wasn't so valuable that time. They'd ramble in any place. Tinkers' asses an' everything that time that'd be going the road used get a place to stay.

'"Well, lookit," says she, "'tis maybe better off you'd be never to bring them three cattle home."

'"Oh God," says he, "I want my cattle."

'"That's your own wishes, now," says she, " but I'm telling you you'd be as well off not to bring 'em home."

'"Well then, I'll bring 'em," he says.

'"All right," says she.

'He went for 'em an' he was two days on the road. He had a long way to go an' he walking, an' as well as that he hadn't the exact place where they were. But he found 'em by asking, anyway, an' brought 'em home. He was home early enough the next evening an' his brother, wasn't he cutting the hay in the field where the cows were to be put. They rose the row. One wanted to put 'em in but the fellow that owned it, he wouldn't have that. An' didn't he put the scythe around his neck an' cut the head of him. So Biddy's words came true when she told him he'd be better off not to bring 'em home.'[118]

Jack Walsh of Flagmount has a further detail to add here:

'They covered him in the field an' waked him in it, where it happened. An' the priest lit the candles around him an' they never quenched all night until they burned out.'

Almost as bad in its outcome, though without any of the gory violence, is the following:

'There was two brothers one time that was beat up bad, an' dying with a dose o' something. The neighbours went to Biddy an' she told 'em – she could see the coffin in the bottle – she told 'em that one of 'em was going to go an' the other one'd recover. An' the one of 'em that was the worst that lived.'[119]

Why did Biddy not specify any further here than she did? Was she trying to be kind, by saving the neighbours from having to break the bad news to one of the brothers? Or could she not tell which brother would live, which die? We will never know.

Another tragic prediction which comes all too true is recounted in this story:

'Long ago there was no lorries or nothing an' they used go to Limerick with pigs in the horse an' car an' creel. But, these two men who knew Biddy well – went to school with her an' danced with her an' all – they went to Limerick with pigs, an' when they were coming back 'twas late. Down by Broadford they'd go, you see, an' back by the Black Sticks, an' they'd go up by Feakle then, in horses an' cars. But Biddy had light an' one lad said,

'"We'll go in to see her."

'"Right," says his companion.

'She had a great welcome for 'em, sure, gave 'em the tea, an' bottles o' stout. Oh, 'twas one o' clock in the morning an' they coming out. They said,

'"We're all right now, an' I hope we'll get home safe."

'"Oh, ye will," she said, "ye will."

'"What do you think of us now?"

'"Oh, you're all right," says she to one of 'em, "an' all your family will prosper, an' that's for sure. An' my words'll come true yet," says she. "Your family will prosper, an' prosper well."

'"An' what about me?" says the other one.

'"I'm sorry to say," says she, "three of your family will go wrong."

'"Ah, don't say that, Biddy. How could that be?"

'"That *will* be," says she. "That day will come. I'm not wishing you any bad luck, but that'll happen you. Three of your family'll lose their mind."

'An' they did. My mother saw 'em in a horse car with a rope tied around 'em, passing her door going into the hospital there above in Ennis. Not the one day, now, but one now an' the other in twelve months time. An' the eldest boy, to escape all this, went abroad. He thought he was right. But he got bad beyond an' he was put into a hospital there.

'An' how well it happened like she said.'[120]

The eldest brother's pathetic effort to reach safety by crossing flowing water is echoed in the next piece, though with happier consequences.

'My father said that his father went to Biddy. 'Tis my father's brother was sick, and she said that he'd be all right, but that he'd have to cross water. And he went to Australia after, an' lived to be an old man there.'[121]

Happy also was the consequence for this young girl who directed Biddy on one of her sick calls, though the happiness was to be tinged with sadness too:

'Sure Biddy was born only a mile an' a half from where my mother was born. An' how my mother met her was this: there was neighbours living in a small little house, a brother an' two sisters – they were old at this time. An' the two sisters were sleeping each side o' the corner, in straw, an' Tom, the brother, had an oul' wooden bed at the other side. But one o' the oul' ladies was done up, an' very badly done up, so Tom walked down all the way for Biddy an' she came next day. But she had fogotten where the house was so she came in to my mother – she was only a slip of a girl – to show her where they lived. An' she went over with her as far as the top o' the hill an' showed her th' oul' house.

'Well, she says to my mother.

'"You'll be married yet," says she, "to a very tall man, an' 'tis all sons you'll have."

'My mother was only laughing. She was only a young slip.

'"How do you know?" says she.

'"'Twill be proved yet," says she. "You'll have six sons, an' you could have the seventh. But you'll have no daughter."

'My mother married my father, Pat O'Brien. He came from Kilanena. An' she had seven sons, two of 'em twins, but the one twin died.

'That's a fact now, then.'[122]

It may seem rather odd that Biddy, who knew so much and such strange information, should have to be told such a simple thing as where a house was, but this is something brought out by many of those who remember her deeds: the future was sometimes a more open book to her than the present. Take the well-known story about the theft of her pig, for example:

'I heard from a man that the fellows that used to be going on *cuaird* there, they stole a pig from her, an' she never found out they stole it. She used to fatten an' kill a pig an' they stole it out o' the house. There was five or six of 'em in it, an' they stole him, an' had him killed an' salted, an' she never found out who stole him.'[123]

Against this set the following:

'A man that came to Biddy looking for a cure one time, she told him all about his own place, the trees around the house an' all that.

'"An'," says she, "since you came here your wife is giving the dinner to a man that called."

'He went home, an' he asked his wife if anything happened while he was away.

'"No," says she.

'"What about the man you gave the dinner to?"

'"Oh, that's right. Our friend Tom Hynes, that didn't call with two years, I gave him the dinner. How did you know that?"

'"'Twas Biddy told me," says he.'[124]

Or consider the following two examples:

'The morning my grandfather an' the other young lads was going to school an' Biddy's house was on fire, didn't one o' the *buachaills* sweep a measure o' whiskey. 'Twas all outside in the yard with the furniture an' all the rest. They took the whiskey, an' going up the road they sat down in the dyke an' drank it. But Biddy never found out they had it gone.'[125]

In the heat of the moment Biddy, no doubt, had things other than whiskey to think of, yet the fact remains that even later she seemed to have no knowledge of the loss – in contrast to the next tale, where she effortlessly foretells a coming event:

'My grandfather was very great with Biddy. But he was working in Bodyke one time, building a farmer's house an' Andy Carey was with him. But didn't they spend until 'twas late in a pub an' it must be all hours o' the morning an' they coming home. Begod, there was light at Biddy's.

'"We'll go up to see her," says he.

'So they did, went up an' in. She said,

'"Hello, Tom," an' knew him well.

'"We came in for a rest."

'"Ye came in for a drink!" says she. "But 'tisn't here, only very little. Whatever is there, ye can have it, but there'll be drink here in half an hour. "'Tis coming," she said, "at Ballinahinch cross. There's two Tipperary men coming to see me."

'An' a while after didn't they land, an' they had a jar o' whiskey.

'"Now ye can drink away," she said to 'em.'[126]

It would seem to be reasonable to deduce from the foregoing and other examples like them that Biddy's special gifts worked for the benefit of others but not for herself. Most people, in fact, believe this to be the case. But how then is the case of the stolen scissors (p. 66) to be explained, or the following, where, seemingly at random she appears not to know one thing but knows another:

'My brother-in-law often told me about his uncle. He went to Biddy an' she told him that there was gold buried in the gable end o' the house, but she was unable to say which gable-end it was. Sure, that was no kind of advice to give. He might have to knock the whole house to get it.'[127]

'A man from Tipperary, he was going on with a court-case over something, maybe land. But 'twas bothering him an' he didn't know whether to continue with it or not. He came to Biddy anyway, an' she told him not to, that he wouldn't come good out of it. So he left it at that, went no farther.'[128]

In the first of these two it could be claimed that there was nothing wrong with Biddy's advice, that it was lack of faith that rendered it useless. If the person had believed, he would, if necessary, have knocked the whole house in the sure knowledge that the gold found would more than cover the cost of rebuilding.

It may be said that the teller of any particular tale will be most likely to remember that one with which he most empathises, or that he will allow his rendering of the facts to be distorted by his own bias. This no doubt has merit as an explanation of some of the above inconsistencies, but will hardly serve as conclusive proof of anything. My own escape from such awkwardness is to plead that my aim is to record what I heard, as I heard it, not to put an end to controversies. That pleasure I willingly relinquish to the reader.

7: Bell, Book and Candle

Remember old Biddy, with her bottle and charm;
She cured all disease in the dull and the fair.
To her cabin they gathered both the noble and gentle
For she was the heroine of sweet County Clare[129]

To most of those who came to her Biddy was indeed a heroine, but
there was one class of men who were not impressed. Or if they were
they succeeded in keeping it a very closely-guarded secret. Reasons
why the priests of the time should have opposed Biddy so vehemently
are not difficult to find. A study of the social history of the latter
half of the nineteenth century can go far to explain it, but since my
space is limited I shall touch only on some of the main issues.

A word from a conversation I had with a man near Feakle may
give a clue to how the warfare between Biddy and the clergy that
was a constant feature of her later career came about. Speaking of
Fr James Dore (parish priest of Feakle 1851-1860) he said,

'Wasn't he the priest that *reigned* in Feakle before Fr Connellan?'

For many of the priests of the time 'reigned' is an appropriate
word, since in a society closed to most outside influences the priest
came to wield a power that was second only to that of the landlord,
and sometimes not even second. His parish was his fiefdom, a reward
for diligent, obedient service, and his interests inevitably spread far
beyond questions of faith and morals, though these continued to
dominate attention. With the boundary between the spiritual and
the temporal so ill defined it was to be expected that some priests
would overstep the mark, and when they did so there were few who
would dare oppose them, in public, at any rate. A comment by a
Tulla man supports this view:

'Our diocese, you see, includes Tipperary, an' we had priests
coming from Tipperary. An' o' course they were very domineering,
the priests o' the past, especially Tipperary men. They were very
wicked.'[130]

Biddy, therefore, if only because of her independence and refusal
to be browbeaten by their authoritarian ways, would sooner or later

have run afoul of them. The fact that she also seemed to dabble with unknown – and therefore, almost by definition, evil – powers marked her out for special attention. But there were other reasons for the conflict too, some excusable, some less so, as we shall see.

In an era of resurgent Catholicism such as the latter half of the nineteenth century, the church of the majority of Irish people was busily trying to shake off the image of a hole and corner organisation serving the needs of illiterate peasants. The great church-building programme of the mid-century is one of the most public facets of this. Further down the line, at parish level, this resurgence took the form of a desire, among priests in particular, to be seen in a good light by those of higher social standing. This need not be seen as mere snobbery. A genuine regard for the public image of the church he represented was a worthy enough concern for a priest. But it could take the form of a narrow authoritarianism, a desire to stamp out all individuality, especially of the kind that might seem to bring unfavourable notice on Catholicism – and such notice was nothing new, as can be seen from some of the literature of the time. It would have been an affront to any self-respecting parish priest to have Biddy, in his parish, giving rise to accusations of peasant witchcraft. In his dealings with his counterparts in the Protestant ministry, for example, he would have been sensible of the scandal given by Biddy's seeming to confirm all the old accusations of 'Popish superstition'.

Also to be taken into account is the social background of the majority of priests. It was not the same as that of Biddy's people. She was of the class of small tenant farmers scarcely above the level of labourers, whereas most priests were the sons of comfortable farmers, a stratum of society that was as modern-minded in matters related to its own advancement as it was conservative in all that concerned land ownership. Such people put their faith – and money – in education as a means of rising in the world. They were only too anxious to leave behind them the half-lit world of peasant lore and herbal medicine. They would not, on the whole, have been sympathetic to Biddy or her ilk.

On a more practical level, if the bishop were to hear too much of this old countrywoman's doings, what might he not say. A priest who could not keep control in his own parish was unlikely to progress much farther through the ranks. And what might be thought of a situation like the following where a parishioner actually challenged her priest:

'Some row she had with the priest in Feakle an' she said one day
to him,

'"If you have power, d'you see that crow that's flying there over-
head? If you can bring down that crow," says she, "I'll pluck him
before he'll reach the ground."

'An' the priest didn't want to use his power, it seems, agin her.
They were in dread of her, like, in a way.'[131]

On what grounds could he confront her, though? Immorality?
Hardly, for even though she was married four times (the last time
in 1869, when she was over seventy years old[132]) there was never
any hint of impropriety, and she had been wed with the blessings
of the Church each time.

Irreligion? No accounts have come down to us that would make
her seem to be either unusually lax or diligent in her performance
of whatever formal duties the Church demanded of her. If, however,
religion is to be measured by the yardstick of practical charity she
could not be found wanting, as we have already seen. Also, it is
often told how her cures were accompanied by the invocation of the
Trinity, and outwardly at least she showed regard for the rosary:

'The oul' lad here, I heard him say he often seen her an' she had
a rosary beads around her neck every day, the cross hanging down,'[133]
though cynics may say she did this merely to allay suspicion.

Scandal? This offered wider possibilities for, to a certain extent
at least, scandal is in the eye of the beholder. One eminently target-
able source of scandal was the never-failing supply of liquor which
she kept and freely dispensed to the neighbouring men who had a
mind to partake. As one man put it for me:

''Twas the greatest house of all for drink. There was no pub as
good as it for the local crowd that had the pluck to go there. There
was whiskey there always.'[134]

Those who went on *cuaird* to Biddy's might have gone to any
other house with impunity, but because of the drink and her reputation their visits there could be seen as anything but innocent pastime.
We have no proof that wives or anyone else actually complained of
Biddy to the priest, but they would not have had to. He had eyes to
see for himself. And if it could be claimed that adults should be
allowed to choose their own company, what about the children?
Was it not imperative to protect them from the poisonous influence
that Biddy spread abroad in the community? Take for example the
case of the boys who stole the whiskey from Biddy the morning her

house was on fire. P. Minogue takes up the tale:

'They sat down, the four of 'em, an' drank the bottle o' whiskey, an' when they arrived in to school, 'twas twelve o'clock. An' master Morrissey was the schoolmaster an' he questioned 'em.

'"What's wrong with ye at all?" he said. He knew they were drunk. But by God, they told him out what had happened. He gave 'em two slaps each an' he told 'em to stay away from Biddy.'

There was little else the master could have done in the circumstances. Most people would have seen the fun in such an incident, but those looking for an excuse to attack Biddy would have found useful ammunition here. To fail to take action was to invite more of the same. And action *was* taken, as one old person near Tulla informed me:

'Biddy had the name of a bad woman. When we went to school, therefore, she was never taught about. We were beaten black an' blue to learn about Brian Merriman, an', sure, there wasn't much difference between his rhymes an' her doings when 'tis all trotted out. There was a headline on the blackboard: BIDDY EARLY WAS A WITCH, an' we were to copy that an' to make the letters like it, you know. That was kind of the policy around Feakle. Nobody much talked about her.'

All this brainwashing of the young was in the future, of course, after her death, but that there was a conspiracy of silence about her in the parish of Feakle during her lifetime is well attested to, as these statements show:

'By God, 'twas nearly a crime to go to her here around, with the priests.'[135]

'Ah, Lord, the old people all believed in Biddy. They'd really adore her only for the priests. They made out she never did any harm to anyone, only the good she done.'[136]

'You'd get more information in Tipperary or Limerick than you would from most people around here. They wasn't afraid of her at all, but the point was that the priest in Feakle, he'd curse anyone that'd go to Biddy. They went to her all right, but 'twas on the sly that they went.'[137]

According to some of the surviving stories what the priest was prepared to resort to was more than mere general threats of cursing. The following is typical:

'The priest used denounce her, you know, an' damn it, sure, when the oul' women'd go to confession he'd ask 'em to know was their husbands going to Biddy's , an' if they said they was, he wouldn't give 'em absolution. The priests didn't want her there at all. They thought if Biddy wasn't in it the people'd be going with five shillings an' ten shillings to theirselves. Now! That was the start of the trouble.'[138]

This latter notion, that the priestly enmity stemmed from financial considerations, is a prevalent one and shows that for all the respect they were held in people were still cynical in their view of clerical motivation. Take this, for example:

'The clergy, of course, she was knocking 'em out of a bit o' money. If you got your leg cured with Biddy you'll give her a bottle o' whiskey, an' maybe you'd go up to himself to say Mass for it if there was no Biddy, you see.'[139]

But on the other hand it must also be said that many believe that the priests did not have to force the people to shun Biddy, as this typical example shows:

'She fell out with the priest in Feakle an' he called her a very wicked woman. An' people over there didn't want to be drawing anything on themselves, for fear they'd have misfortune, you know.'[140]

Whatever the means by which it came about, a pall of silence, a desire by most people to forget about Biddy, seems to have been the order of the day after her death:

'After she dying there wasn't ever a whole lot talked about her around here. All this started only in these late years.'[141]

That this silence had done its work is suggested by the next comment:

'We weren't so curious about Biddy as we grew up. All the curious queries an' everything have come up in the late times, you know.'[142]

However, while she lived and was able to give comfort to the troubled, cures to the afflicted, the crowds continued to come to her in spite of anything the clergy might say. Even priests themselves, it seems, were not above consulting her in private, whatever might be their public stance:

'Oh, the priests called her all kinds o' names off o' the altar, an' still they used to come to her dressed up as ordinary men. They did, begod.'[143]

'Faith, it was known that the priests came there in covered buggies to her, priests that was done up, so they wouldn't be seen.'[144]

Even the parish priest of Feakle, her arch-enemy in the stories, was forced to avail himself of her power, if we are to believe the surviving accounts:

'Herself an' the priest in Feakle didn't get on. He was telling people to keep away from her, an' they were only going unknown to him. They didn't want him to know they were going. An' 'twas said he went to her after, himself, to get cured, that he was dying of cancer, an' that she cured him.'[145]

The arguments will continue, no doubt, the outcome depending largely on personal spleen or goodwill towards one side or the other. But what seems equally sure is that the story of the priest's horse will continue to be told wherever Biddy is remembered. It is by far the most popular tale associated with her memory and I have found more clear and vivid versions of it than of any other. The first version shows the priest about his legitimate business, but walking into trouble unsuspectingly. This version differs from the others in that there is only a slight suggestion that Biddy was to blame for the accident. She is seen more in the light of a prospective helper who has to be cajoled because of past insults to her:

'You see, the priests was up against her for one reason or another. But, somewhere between Feakle an' Tulla where there's trenches along the road – it could be around Ayle – it happened with a hunt. There were packs o' beagles from Tulla an' Feakle an' several other parishes hunting, an' the priest was coming along on a sick call on horseback. An' previous to this he had gave her a lacerating – I don't know whether 'twas off the altar or that she heard that he gave her a bit of a tonguing, but I declare to God, as the horse was passing this place, the hare had passed an' the hounds came out through the fence, out on the road, frightened the horse, an' he went into a trench at th' other side. The huntsmen came along – they'd be on foot after the dogs. The priest, o' course, was wet, an' he came out on the road. They all gathered around the horse then, but if they tried their endeavours best, what men was in it, they couldn't bring the horse up out o' the trench. So someone suggested that the only hope for the horse was to go for Biddy. O' course, 'twasn't easy for the priest to say "I'll go myself." A messenger went for Biddy, anyway, and when he went in she knew, the same as if you had her told, what was wrong.

'"I know," she says. "Go back now an' tell himself to come."

'So he had to humble himself an' come for her himself. An' she went back, an' all she did, they said, was take a scollop out of the fence, an' hit the horse back on the neck, an' up he hopped, up on the road.

'So the following Sunday, or whenever he was on the altar again, he said she was a useful woman in the country. He had to eat his words, like.'[146]

There are variations of course. Sometimes the priest who is punished is from Tipperary, sometimes from Feakle, but all agree in broad outline that he was well and truly put in his place. I have said in the introduction that I believe this story's popularity to be due to some unconscious (or all too conscious?) desire on the part of people to see respected but often disliked figures brought low in a way that did no essential damage to themselves or the popular institution they represented (as many people nowadays take delight in seeing a political party leader making a fool of himself now and again, while at the same time slackening not a whit in support for the party he represents).

In the next version the priest is more specifically coming to talk to Biddy about the errors of her ways when he comes to grief. Her scathing reference to him as a 'so-called priest' may tell us that her dislike was not so much directed against the office of priesthood but against those occupants of the office who failed, in her opinion, to live up to it. To her, persons in authority were to be respected only if deserving of respect.

'Now some time after Biddy getting married to Tom Early when she went to Kilbarron the priests of Feakle started denouncing her an' abusing her. They made out that she was a witch an' a fairy for what she was doing. But, above Kilbarron there was a bog called Ayle bog, an' there was a trench out o' the bog going into Kilbarron lake an' 'twas going under the road a short distance from Biddy's house. An' it appears that both ends o' this stretch were on the same level. The water that was in it was dead water; there was no flow either way in it. But in the winter-time the lake would rise, an' of course if the bogwater rose, the trench, 'twould rise up on the road near Biddy's house an' there might be two or three feet o' water in the road. But at the time I'm talking about 'twas about the end o' November an' there was very heavy rain, an' the road was flooded.

'An' there was a priest in Feakle an' he heard about Biddy. But he left Feakle one day after his dinner, an' at that time the priests, if they were only going a hundred yards, 'tis on horseback they'd go. But this priest, he had a horse, an' he brought the horse, o' course, from Feakle.

'Anyway, he set out for Biddy's. An' the flood was up on the road a short distance from her house, hardly the eighth of a mile. An' he had a cane for hitting the horse to make him go. But when he was going right in the middle o' the flood the horse stood on the road an' the priest above on his back. He beat the horse trying to make him go, an' he might as well be hitting the water the horse was outside in. He was there about an hour when another man came along the road riding on another horse. He pulled up by the side o' the priest an' he asked him what was wrong.

'"How do I know?" says the priest to him. "The horse won't go for me. An' might I ask you," says he, "where you're going?"

'"I'm going over to Biddy Early," says he, "for a cure for my brother that's sick."

'"For God's sake," says the priest, "will you keep away from her because she's a witch, a definite witch."

'"Begod," says the man to him, "she has thousands cured an' I don't see why she wouldn't cure my brother."

'"Oh, go away, so," says the priest to him.

'Your man told the horse to go on. The horse went on the road, an' after he going the priest hit his horse a wallop again to know would he make him go. Sure, the horse wouldn't move.

'The other man went over to Biddy. He went in to her an' when he went in,

'"How in the name o' goodness are you, John Hegarty?" she said to him.

'"How did you know me?" says the man to her.

'"I knew you," says she, "the minute you left your own house. An' you have come here to me now for a cure for your brother that's sick. An' when you were coming the road," says Biddy to him, "there was another fellow there beyond, a so-called priest, in the middle of a flood o' water above on a horse's back, coming over," says she, "to denounce me an' abuse me for what I was doing, curing the people of their ailments. Will you go back now, John Hegarty, when you're going home," says she to him, "an' tell that fellow that's in the flood o' water to let me alone or if he don't I'll make it tough for him. I can leave him in the flood o' water for a week if I like. When he tells you," says she, " that he promises that he's going to have no more to do with me I'll let him go. An' where he'll go is not over here to me, but back to Feakle, an' there he can let me alone for the future. An' if he thinks," says she, "to come over to me again I'll put him in the way that he won't be able to. Go back now an' tell him that. An' here is a bottle for your brother," says she. "Tell your brother to take three spoonfuls out o' the bottle. Three days, now, one day after the other, in the morning, give him three spoonfuls out o' the bottle, an' the third day he'll be perfect."

'So John Hegarty took the bottle, whatever she had in it, an' he went back to the priest. He told him what Biddy told him an' the priest promised him there an' then that he'd have no more to do with Biddy, only leave her alone. An' as soon as he promised that to John Hegarty he was let go an' he turned around his horse an' went back to Feakle an' never troubled Biddy after.'[147]

It may be said here in passing that the motif of the man stuck to the horse is an old one. Take for example the story of the *Giolla Deacair* from the Fenian cycle of tales.

In the following we see, if not sympathy for the priest, at least an excuse for his actions – he may have been innocent about what he was getting himself into by taking on Biddy!

'The priest gave out about Biddy at the people, that 'twasn't right to be going near her, or looking for requests from her or anything. But when he was going home in his pony an' trap the pony jumped into an oul' trench. Now, there was men, an' strong men that time, an' none of 'em could stir the pony out of it. Some smart man, that wasn't going to take any soft talk from anyone, he said.

'"Listen, Father. By the way the business is going on here, now," he said, "we're not able to bring up that pony, nor he won't stir out of it. I think you said too much today."

'"Maybe I did," said the priest.

'"I think you did," he said. "An' excuse me, now, but there's something wrong. You'll have to go to Biddy."

'"Would you go for me?"

'"Well, I will," he said, "but it must be at your request."

'"Yes, it is," the priest said.

'He couldn't bear to go back himself, but the lad went back. An' the boys knew it well, that he done too much talking, because they had a belief of Biddy, that she was no harm to anyone an' that she was helpful. But he mightn't be long in Feakle, an' when he heard of her he got very annoyed an' said he'd give this sermon.

'The lad came in anyway, an' he told her the story.

'"I know," says she. "Well, as he has so much to say about me today" – an' she wasn't at Mass at all, you know – "an' the harm I can do, isn't it a wonder he couldn't take out the pony. You can go away now," says she, "an' he'll be all right."

'Whatever she did, the pony make a plunge up, an' they had only to give him a small little hand an' he pulled up on the road. The priest knew then. As soon as he asked her permission to release the pony, it was done.'[148]

One account puts the event in a much more public setting, with even the bishop present:

'There was a priest one time an' he was terrible agin her, a parish priest. An' he was always cutting her out o' the altar an' doing the devil on her. But the bishop – I think he was McRedmond that was here in this diocese one time – he was confirming childer someplace, an' they all came from all around to meet him. An' Biddy was in it.

'This bishop was moving off to another parish, anyway, an' there was a funeral o' sidecars after him. The oul' priests had all sidecars, you know, an' a man driving 'em. An' when this priest thought to start his horse he wouldn't start. An' all the parishioners was around this horse trying to make him go, an' someone says,

'"Wouldn't ye call Biddy Early" – she was in the crowd. She came over an' got a twig, gave the horse a tip, an' she said to the priest,

'"Why wouldn't you make him go now," says she, "out of all your power?" hitting him a tip o' the twig, an' off he went.

'He never said a word about her after.'[149]

A very similar story to this was told to me (also in Kilkishen) about a priest who was to be silenced because of alcoholism, and who greeted the bishop who came to silence him by sticking his carriage to the road.

The most graphic account of all is of the Tipperary priest who sought to achieve by threats of physical violence what his fellow-clergymen had failed to enforce by persuasion:

'There was people coming up to her from Tipperary, an' this priest down there heard where they were off to. So he put his saddle on the black mare he had, an' he went on as well as the rest, up to where she lived. An' he called her out. She came out an' she leaned over the little half-door. Anyway, he threatened her – he had a big whip – an' he came to the half-door.

'"Look, Biddy, you'll have to leave here. You're destroying my parish with people coming to you."

'"I'm doing no harm, Father," says Biddy.

'"Well, I'll make you leave. An' if you're here when I come again, I'll give you the whip."

'"Take your time, now," says she. "You're not at home at all yet."

'Anyway, he came out an' he went up on the horse, came out along, an' went up Annasallagh, a narrow road. An', begor, going up near a bridge didn't the horse fall out on top of his head, an' the priest fell at one side an' the horse at the other. The next thing was, the priest was stuck to the ditch. An' there did a little Johnny Murphy come down the hill.

'"Oh," says the priest, "I'm glad someone to come."

'"Why, Father?"

'"Oh, that villain below has me stuck to the ditch. Will you run down to her, an' if she can do anything, tell her to do it an' I'll never trouble her again."

'Poor oul' Johnny ran – an' he had a mile to go or more – an' he went in to her an' he said,

'"Lookit, Biddy, you have him dead above on the side of the road."

'"Ah, the Devil sure to him, if he left me alone I wouldn't touch him."

'"Do something for him anyway."

'"I declare I will, this time."

'But she got a little bottle, an' whether 'twas the little man she put into it or what, she gave it to Johnny.

'"When you go up, now, shake it three times over him, an' I bet you he'll stir an' rise up."

'An' begor, he did. Dhera, as soon as he got a drop out o' the bottle he jumped up.

'"Thank you, Johnny," says he, "but I'll never go near the villain again."'[150]

Here the priest's helplessness is, no doubt, a punishment to match his own violent behaviour. Little could he have known that his threat to move her by force would have dredged up memories for Biddy from the year 1816 when Sheehy had promised to do the same thing, and had been warned in the same way by her. Note also that the release is effected here by a bottle, whereas in other versions a piece of twig etc. is used – sometimes accompanied by an invocation of the Trinity, as in this:

'She went out anyway, an' she pulled two rushes. She said,

'"Do that now," – made the sign of the cross – "with the two rushes. Put it to the horse's breast when you go back, an' he'll move then."'[151]

Finally, a version that contains not alone the episode of the priest's punishment but also some of the features we have seen in other chapters:

'There was a man above from Ballard, he had a horse, an' he was a valuable horse. Good horses were scarce in those days, you know. An' the horse got sick. An' honest to God, didn't somebody recommend him to go to Biddy Early. He did. He got down there all right, an' I declare to God, he was only just down below when who did he meet but the priest. Well, the priest didn't believe in Biddy at all, you know. An' the priest knew that he was a stranger.

'"Where are you coming from?" he says.

'"A place called Ruan," he says.

'"An' where are you going?"

'"I'm going to see a woman," says he, "to cure a horse for me."

'"Lookit, my good man, will you go home an' mind your own business. That horse'll die," he says, "an' you have a journey done for nothing."

'"Well, by God, Father," he says, "as I came down I'll go to see her anyway."

'An' he was only inside the gate at her house but she says,

'"The holy man came at you?"

'"He did, ma'am," says your man, "but 'tis no good for him."

'"Well, I'll deal with that fellow," she says, "before long."

'She gave him whatever she had to give him for the horse, an' she says he'd be going crossing a bridge – that was Drumcanora bridge below there –

'"You'll be crossing a bridge on your way home an' the horse'll shy," she says. "But if you can hold above on him the horse'll be all right when you get home."

'An' when he was going out she seen him out to the gate, an' wasn't the priest coming up, an' didn't his horse get stuck to the road, the priest's horse. An' he was bucking over it, you see, having to ask her to free him.

'"My good woman," says he, "could you do something for me?"

'"Well, you prevented me from doing something for other people," she says, "an' you'll stop there now until that fellow gets home."

'Bejasus, he was there for the most of a day. But he got out of it eventually when she let him off. And, when the lad from Ruan came home the horse was improved, an' he did whatever he had to do with the cure, you see, an' there wasn't a bit wrong with the horse after that.'[152]

In this telescoped version of many of the other stories we see an aggressive Biddy, making a spectacle of the priest. If this was what happened, human nature alone might prompt the priest's lasting enmity – a grudge that would be remembered when Biddy, on her deathbed, needed a priest. On that occasion, some accounts tell, he would not consent to give her the sacrament until she handed over her bottle, a symbolic act in the circumstances.

As I have said previously in this chapter the clergy may have had little success in smothering Biddy's fame during her lifetime – their efforts, on the contrary, tended only to increase it – but after her death their endeavours seemed to be more fruitful and the memory of her deeds abated. But at no time was it forgotten, and people who were born only at the beginning of this century, thirty years or more after her death, still stand up fiercely for her today, will not hear a word spoken against her, as though she were one of their own family:

'People were telling me that she was a bad woman, that she was married four times an' all that. I didn't care, says I, if she was married forty times. She never did a bad turn to anyone, an' that's all that matters.'[153]

'A fellow was arguing it out with me in the bog. "Oh," says he, "she couldn't have power. God didn't give power to His own mother."

'"Well," says I, "'tis by the sign o' the cross she used to cure. Joan of Arc," says I, "was burned at the stake an' she freed her country, an' sure, didn't they hang Our Lord an' he curing people. Not comparing poor Biddy to Him, like, but isn't that what you get," says I, " for doing the good turn. She was supposed to be a witch, an' sure, Joan of Arc was a witch too. St Kevin was a witch too, the oul' king told him when he turned the seven sons into seven churches there in Glendalough. D'you ever hear that? There's seven churches in Glendalough. This oul' king, he had a pet gander an' the gander died. So he sent for the saint to know could he bring him to life, cure him. He said he would.

'"But," says he, "you'll have to promise me that you'll give me as much land as he'll be able to fly around when I have him brought to life, for I want to build on it, before I cure him."

'So the oul' king signed it up that he would. An' didn't the gander fly thirty miles around. An' the king went violent. He went to do away with him. He made out he was a witch. He vexed St Kevin. An' he had seven sons, an' Kevin turned 'em into seven churches, an' they're still there in Glendalough."'[154]

Anyone who can evoke such comment, provoke such comparison, a century later, deserves to be remembered among the immortals, for better or worse.

8: Rest in Peace?

One might expect that many verifiable factual details about Biddy's later life should survive. After all, times had improved since her birth at the turn of the eighteenth century and she had acquired a wide-ranging reputation and much notoriety. Yet her final years are almost as bereft of fact as is her youth. Part of the problem is that in the folk-memory all the instances of cures and foretelling are lumped together with scant regard for chronology. This is, no doubt, a true reflection of how the human mind works, but unfortunately it is liable to leave gaping holes even in what should be a simple account of the main facts of a person's life.

However, a certain amount *is* known: that she appeared in court in Ennis in 1865 charged with witchcraft;[155] that she was married a fourth time late in life; that she died poor; that she ended her days in Kilbarron. This is indeed the sketchiest of outlines, yet little more than this survives that can definitely be dated in the thirty-odd years between her marriage to Tom Flannery in the early 1840s and her death in 1874.

Then suddenly (as before in the case of her cures), a flood of light scatters this darkness when we come to her last illness and death. These few days are etched as clearly on the people's memory as the preceding three decades are glossed over lightly. Yet if one were to ask when, precisely, did she die the chances are that no one would be able to come reasonably near to the year, or even the decade. Obviously, it is the dramatic situation that has appealed to the people rather than such abstractions as dates. What, after all, can be said about day and year except to state them. On the other hand, a whole hour's entertainment, a very lesson in understanding of human character, can be built up from the details of what happened at the last confrontation of Biddy and the priest, those two representatives of powers that were considered to be so much at odds but which may have been, in the end, one and the same. Of such situations are legends made, and legends, more than mere cold facts, are what the human imagination thrives on. And who is to say that the poeple's way of remembering is any less useful or authentic than that practised by more scientific historians? In the end which of them tells us more

about people and what they hold most dear? Certainly there is no
room for the despising of one by the other, as has, up to now, been
too often the case. We are indeed lucky that in the matter of Biddy
the memory of her death survives among the people, since without
it we would have nothing. Documentary history, until very recently,
had little place for such lowly people as her, since those who wrote
such history would, by their very background and training, have
been almost bound to ignore her.

*   *   *   *   *

The first fact, chronologically speaking, that I discovered about
her last years is one concerning her last marriage:
  'Biddy was married to an O'Brien from Limerick, you know. He
was the last man she married. He came to her sick an' she cured
him. She said,
  '"If I cure you will you marry me?"
  '"I will," he said – he was a young fellow. An' she *did* cure him,
an' he *did* marry her. His family was from Newcastlewest.'[156]
  There is some dispute about the actual name of this husband, the
newspapers reporting it as O'Brien, the marriage records having it
as Meaney,[157] but the important thing, from my point of view, is
that a memory of the fact remains. Why she should have married
someone who was very much younger than herself when it was
obvious that the disparity in their ages would provoke hostile comment, perhaps mockery, certainly accusations of witchcraft, is hard
to tell. Maybe after her long marriage to Tom Flannery she felt she
needed someone close to her, to care for her in her declining years.
Like so much else, we can only guess at her motives. Perhaps she no
longer regarded what people said about her, knowing that those
who were ill-disposed to her would talk in any case, and that a
fourth marriage was unlikely to alienate those friends who had stood
by her through thick and thin, friends such as Pat Loughnane and
Tom Minogue. They it was who in April 1874, when Biddy was ill,
came to the conclusion that no matter what her past disagreements
with the clergy might have been she deserved to have the rites of the
church at her passing. Perhaps even they harboured lingering doubts
as to the source of her powers and the possible consequences for her
in the next world.
  Biddy herself must have realised she would not survive this illness

because she sent for Pat Loughnane, and what she said to him displays a clear knowledge on her part that this was the end of the road, and that there was a very little business only to be attended to:

'My grandfather, oul' Pat Loughnane, was supposed to be a great man, one o' the best that ever came into Feakle. But it seems he used to bury a lot o' people for nothing, people that couldn't pay – he had an undertaking, you know. An' Biddy, it seems, had no money, an' when she was bad she sent for Pat. An' she said to him,

'"Will you bury me?"

'"I will," says Pat.

'"Well, you can have my haggart if you do, an' the house."'[158]

Here we see clearly that Biddy was poor to the last. She had abided by the condition laid on her when she first got the bottle, and the result was poverty for herself though she had given comfort to thousands who had come to her through the years. Hopefully she regarded the bargain as having been a worthwhile one.

Biddy's last evening and night in this world (21-2 April, 1874) are vividly remembered, as the detail of the following account shows:

'Pat Loughnane an' a man by the name o' Minogue, they lived there in Kilbarron, you know. But they said she shouldn't be let die without the priest, they'd chance going for the priest. So they got some young neighbour boy, an' he went for the priest to Feakle, the curate. An' he got his man an' tackled up a horse an' sidecar, an' came down. The man stopped outside, minding the horse, an' the priest came in. An' there was a lamp there on the wall, you see, lighting, a paraffin-oil lamp. An' there was a candle lighting inside in Biddy's room where she was dying, an' when the priest approached, that lamp quenched an' the light inside in the room quenched, the candle. So he put his hand in his pocket – I suppose he used to smoke – an' cracked a match an' he lit the candle again. An' it quenched again. So he said the prayers then over Biddy from the mouth. He couldn't read the dying prayers at all; he had no light. 'Twas pure dark. He just said the prayers that he had to mind.

'So he went away then, an' one o' the men spoke over to her,

'"How are you, Biddy?"

'She muttered something, anyway. But after a while's time again, then, they were at the fire, an' from her room, out here to the door, a kind o' ball o' fire came out, an' went out the front door. One o' the men went up an' he lit the lamp an' he said,

'"Are you all right, Biddy?"

'No answer. He looked down at the other man.

'"Is she dead?"

'"She could be. Go in an' see," says he.

'He went in anyway, an' he lit the candle inside from a match, an' she was stone dead in the bed. That was the finish o' Biddy. She was stone dead.'[159]

This account make no mention of the bottle but carries conviction in the mood of silence it builds up in that little house as darkness gathered for the last time about Biddy. It is tempting to see the ball of fire that proceeded from the death-room to the door as her soul, free at last of the old worn-out body, making its way to freedom.

However, by far the most popular account of her death brings in some mention of the bottle and what happened to it. This next is typical:

'Biddy was sick an' very bad. Now I can't tell you whether 'twas the way this parish priest was sent for or that he heard about her being sick, but anyway he went to the house when she was in bed, an' he went into the room to hear her confession. An' where he was hearing her confession at the back o' the house, there was a big ash tree outside, an' generally nearly in all the old houses there were very small windows. But the small window, anyway, was at the back o' the room, an' facing the tree. An' there was a crow outside in the tree an' the crow having Caw! Caw! Caw! all the time while the priest was hearing her confession.

'But after the confession Biddy says to him,

'"Father," says she, "could you bring in that crow to the end o' the bed?"

'"I'll try, anyway," says he.

'He started to pray an' read out of a book. The crow was all the time outside in the tree having Caw! Caw! Caw! out of him. But when the priest finished reading out o' the book,

'"I'll bring her in," says Biddy.

'She sat up in the bed an' she lifted up the pillow an' took out her magic bottle from under it. An' whatever she said, or whatever she did, the back window was open an' the crow flew in an' perched on the end o' the bed an' started to Caw! Caw! Caw! Biddy says to the priest,

'"That's what you couldn't do, now. Will you put out the crow now?" says she to him again.

'He started to pray an' pray. The crow started on the end o' the bed, Caw! Caw! Caw! all the time.

'"Well, I'll put her out," says Biddy.

'She held the bottle out in her hand with the neck of it facing the crow, an' the crow flew out the window again an' up on the tree an' started Caw! Caw! Caw! above in the tree again.

'She gave the bottle to the priest.

'"There 'tis for you, now," says she, "an' you'll have the same powers as I had."

'But what did the priest do with it only threw it into Kilbarron lake, an' 'tis supposed to be there yet.'[160]

If we are to believe this, Biddy had lost none of her old fire and her challenge to the clergy was kept up right until the end. Some may find it unbelievable that a person at death's door would be so preoccupied with such seemingly petty point-scoring, but the notion of contests or trials of strength or skill have a hallowed place in the memory of the people. In Biddy's own area, Feakle, they were nothing new. Stories of the infamous *Conchúir Thaidhg* and his challenges to the priest of the parish were well known during Biddy's lifetime, and there is good reason for believing that some of the reputed doings of Biddy herself are based on the model of *Conchúir*. In spite of any such borrowing, however, it is still remarkable that two figures, both unconventional and possessed of uncanny powers, should have originated from and worked in the same area.

Stories of challenges between nineteenth century hedge-school-masters are widespread not only in Clare but all over Ireland, and within living memory there is the case of Fr Frawley, still spoken of with reverence in the Sixmilebridge area, who when he first came to the parish challenged the old parish priest to a trial of their respective powers. He, by his prayers, was able to light the altar-candles from a distance of thirty feet, whereas the older man could only make them smoulder.

If such contests seem childish to a modern audience perhaps they should be looked at in the way that they were meant to be seen, that is as a way of asserting the self, an older form of advertising, one might say. That they provided memorable entertainment for onlookers or hearers is also undoubtedly true.

In none of the accounts that survive is there mention of a wake for Biddy. Was this because she was now living alone again, her fourth husband having predeceased her? Where were her relatives? No mention of them survives. To the very end the focus is on herself alone and her bottle.

Take herself first. Her passing was a quiet one. After all the droves of people she had cured, only a handful were present to see her off. The fact that she had made her peace with the priest would not have had time to be much known, and after the enmity of half a lifetime most people were not willing to have their presence at the funeral misunderstood.

'There was only six people to walk over in her funeral the day she was burying. That was all. Oul' William Connors that lived there beyond, he walked over, for he was a very intelligent man an' he considered Biddy was doing no harm to anyone.

'People weren't told to stay away, but for fear the priest'd think that they was in cope with her. The priests that was ruling the parishes in them times, you could do nothing with 'em. If you took one step out o' place the parish priest was after you.'[161]

One of those present, Daniel Minogue, was only a child at the time. He mitched from school especially for the occasion and was all his life proud that he had done so. Perhaps it was his way of repaying her for her kindness, for the slices of bread and jam that she had so often given him.

Some accounts have it that many priests were present at the funeral, but this seems hardly credible, unless they came out of curiosity, or out of a desire to disperse expected large crowds of mourners. I find myself much more convinced by the picture of the coffin followed by the little group.

She was buried in Feakle churchyard, not far from the grave of Brian Merriman and though no gravestone marks her final resting place and the exact spot is the subject of argument there are people yet who will undertake with confidence to point it out:

'Well, Thady Kelly showed me her grave one time; in 1928, it was. An' he was an old man that time. He never remembered her himself, but he knew her grave. There was an ash tree on the road down to Kelly's an' just about ten paces from that tree he showed it to me.'[162]

And so, at last, she was gone. Right-thinking people could breathe easily again now that a prime source of wickedness was out of the way. The priest in Feakle (Fr Connellan) must have been feeling positively lighthearted, if the next account is to be believed:

'The priest that used criticise her, he made a sermon in Feakle after Biddy dying, an' he referred to her as being a great, wonderful, charitable, good woman. Anything she ever did was for the good. – "We never heard o' her doing anything bad to anybody" – an' 'twasn't he was against her at all while she was alive, but other priests. An' he referred to how the priests was criticising her. But, he said "She was as good, an' maybe better, than us." Them are the words he said in Feakle the Sunday after her death.'[163]

Perhaps he was trying to be charitable; perhaps her death had given him a new perspective on the problem that had been Biddy. But his audience will no doubt have given each other sideways glances, some of them suppressing the desire to smile. Most might have said 'We could have told you so a long time ago.'

Her bottle deserves special mention since it has mesmerised generation after generation since her death. Most old people held the probably sensible view that it was usable only by Biddy herself, that in other hands it would be of no more value than any ordinary bottle. This has in no way diminished the desire to find it, though, and the fact that its resting place could be so closely pinpointed made it merely a matter of time before desire became translated into practical efforts to find it. The story of these gropings at the bottom of Kilbarron lake needs no retelling here, especially since the bottle may have been long gone, anyway:

'But 'twas supposed the priest threw it into Kilbarron lake. Dhera, whoever owned it might take it back again. Sure, we don't know which. They even put divers into the lake to try to find it. They found lots o' bottles, but they didn't know whether they had the right one or not, anyway, when they weren't able to work it, o' course.'[164]

The feeling that the bottle was only on loan to Biddy is apparent here, and also in other accounts (for example 'Once she died the bottle was never heard of from that out. Back to 'Themselves' it went, I suppose').[165] But it may not be quite true to say that it was never seen from the time of her death on. In the next story, its being thrown into the lake had an odd sequel:

'You heard that the priest threw the bottle into the lake, didn't you? Well, some time after there did some stranger come, an' he met somebody in Feakle an' he asked them would they be able to show him Kilbarron lake. They couldn't at the time, but there was a man there sitting on the window – he was a tailor – an' he was finishing off work middling early an' he was only looking for something to pass away the evening, so he came with him an' he showed him the lake. So they stood at the brow o' the lake for a while an' the next thing there was this swishing noise, an' this thing came along the water. An' he snapped it into his pocket an' poor man got one squint at it, that 'twas a blue bottle, but he didn't let him see any more. He only just got one squint at it. But he thought it was the real one anyway, for it came along the lake of its own accord to him whatever power he had – he might be some relation or something. He pocketed it, anyway, in a shot. Says he "I have nothing to give you now, but some day you'll be surprised at yourself."

'He went away then but he told him an' he going that whatever he'd get would never get any smaller. So all went well, an' there was no sign of anything happening, but one morning the tailor got up, an' it was in the dark nearly – he used get up early – an' he couldn't get the trousers on him. So he lit some kind of a light, an' he loosened up the trousers, an' there was rolls upon rolls o' money stuck in it. He couldn't put the trousers on him with the money so he went to the bank with it, lodging it, an' the manager nearly fainted. But he lodged it, anyway, an' 'twas a colossal amount o' money in those days.

'But your man had told him that 'twould never grow smaller, even if he drew from it itself. Supposing he had £500, 'twould be still £500 if he took £200 out of it.

'But he died three months after, but 'twas there for his family. Although I knew a grandson an' he didn't seem to have any of it.

''Twas an old man o' ninety years that told me that story.'[166]

Who was this purposeful stranger and what was it that he found in the lake? The teller's speculation that he may have been a relative could be close to the mark. But a relative by blood or by power? The promise he made to the tailor is reminiscent of what Biddy herself might have uttered and the consequences for the tailor certainly suggest that here indeed was some power out of the ordinary at work, more than likely that of the Good People.

In all these accounts, no matter how the details may vary, the reader will be struck by their similarity to the legend of the mysterious Lady of the Lake claiming back the good servant, Excalibur, when its master was no longer alive to use it, carrying into the murky depths (of the human mind as much as the lake-bottom) an object that had betokened hope in grim times for a people hard pressed by the surrounding darkness.

It is a suitable note to conclude on, for it seems certain that as long as Biddy is remembered mystery will surround her, not the obvious tantalising questions whose answers merely escape us, such as when/where did she get the bottle? Where precisely is she buried? Where is the bottle now? Why did the drawer of her dresser that contained the bottle disappear?, but the deeper questions to which there may be no answers in this world, questions like: Where did her power come from? Who chose her, and why?

Long after all the other details have ceased to matter she herself will still be there, standing on the edge of our consciousness, on the edge of our visible world, touching also another, smiling ruefully at our ignorance of the dark, daring us to believe.

Notes

1. P. J. O'Halloran, Tyreragh, Tulla
2. Paddy McMahon, Rathclooney, Crusheen
3. Johnny Broderick, Derrybrien
4. Frank O'Brien, Doora, Ennis
5. Jimmy Armstong, Ballyroughan, Quin
6. Frank O'Brien
7. Paddy Minogue, Ayle, Feakle
8. P. Minogue, Derrananeal, Feakle
9. *ibid*
10. Paddy Floyd, Affick, Tulla
11. Thomas Hannon, Flagmount
12. Paddy Shannon, Doolin
13. Jimmy Armstrong
14. Johnny Broderick
15. Jim Daffy, Crusheen
16. Dan Ryan, Knockjames, Tulla
17. James Torpey, Scariff
18. Bridget Dinan, Maghera, Tulla
19. P. J. O'Halloran
20. Frank O'Brien
21. Johnny Broderick
22. Tom Daly, Ardane, Kilkishen
23. Thomas Hannon
24. Tomo Scanlan, Ceathrú na Cloiche, Crusheen
25. P. J. O'Halloran
26. Johnny Broderick
27. Paddy Minogue
28. Bridget Dinan
29. P. Minogue
30. Martin Commane, Newhall, Ennis
31. Lady Gregory, *Visions and Beliefs in the West of Ireland*, Colin Smythe, 1970, p. 34.
32. Tom Daly
33. Liam Loughnane, Cranaher, Tulla. See also Lady Gregory, *Visions and Beliefs in the West of Ireland*, p. 38
34. Tom Daly
35. Paddy McMahon
36. P. Murphy, Tubber
37. Tom O'Donoghue, Port, Ruan
38. Jimmy Armstrong
39. Paddy Minogue
40. Martin Commane
41. Johnny Broderick

42. Dan Ryan
43. Johnny Broderick
44. Dan Ryan
45. P. J. O'Halloran
46. Dan Ryan
47. Tomo Scanlan
48. Paddy Shannon
49. Paddy Floyd
50. Paddy Shannon
51. Joe Murphy, Tyreragh, Tulla
52. T. Pyne, Ruan
53. Carolyn White, *A History of Irish Fairies*, Mercier Press, 1976, p. 54; see also Lady Gregory, *Visions and Beliefs in the West of Ireland*, pp. 250-54
54. Tom Daly
55. Dan Ryan
56. Tom Daly
57. Dan Ryan
58. P. Minogue
59. Liam Loughnane
60. Mrs Sheehan, Manusmore, Clarecastle
61. Frank O'Brien
62. *ibid*
63. Kevin Danaher, *The Year in Ireland*, Mercier Press, 1972, pp. 109-19
64. Dan Ryan
65. *ibid*
66. P. Minogue
67. Jack Walsh, Flagmount
68. Molly McMahon, Toberbreeda, Crusheen
69. Thomas Hannon
70. P. J. O'Halloran
71. Recorded at Naughton's, Kilclaran, Feakle
72. James Nash, Tulla
73. Martin Commane
74. John J. Fitzgibbon, Crusheen
75. Mrs O'Loughlin, Dysert O'Dea
76. Dan Casey, Ruan
77. Paddy Guthrie, Moyree, Ruan
78. Paddy Shannon
79. Tom Daly
80. Recorded in Peterswell, Co. Galway
81. Bridget Dinan
82. P. J. O'Halloran
83. Joe Murphy
84. Jimmy Armstrong
85. Jack Walsh
86. James Torpey

87. P. Murphy
88. Jimmy Armstrong
89. James Nash
90. Tom Daly
91. Thomas Hannon
92. Molly McMahon
93. James Nash
94. Johnny Broderick
95. Tom Daly
96. Jack Walsh
97. Johnny Broderick
98. Thomas Hannon
99. Jack Walsh
100. Johnny Broderick
101. Mrs O'Connor, Kilanena
102. *ibid*
103. Many legal disputes involving neighbours will, on investigation, be found to have their origins in suspicions of piseóg-working, but this rarely comes out in court.
104. Mrs Hanrahan, Barntick, Clarecastle
105. Molly McMahon
106. P. Minogue
107. Dan Ryan
108. Jimmy O'Connor, Tubber
109. *Smearachán*: a small, mean-spirited person
110. Johnny Broderick
111. Jack Walsh
112. Joe Murphy
113. Molly McMahon
114. Bridget Dinan
115. John Nagle, Ballyheeragh
116. Martin Commane
117. Jimmy Long, Ballinahinch
118. P. Murphy
119. Tom Daly
120. Frank O'Brien
121. Mrs O'Loughlin
122. Frank O'Brien
123. Michael Hanrahan, Barntick, Clarecastle
124. Mrs Sheehan
125. P. Minogue
126. Thomas Hannon
127. Liam Loughnane
128. Mrs Sheehan
129. P. J. O'Halloran
130. Paddy Floyd
131. Liam Loughnane

132. Meda Ryan, *Biddy Early: The Wise Woman of Clare*, Mercier Press, 1978, p. 87
133. P. Minogue
134. Joe Murphy
135. P. Minogue
136. Joe Murphy
137. Jack Walsh
138. P. Minogue
139. P. J. O'Halloran
140. Liam Loughnane
141. P. Minogue
142. Paddy Floyd
143. P. Minogue
144. Tom Daly
145. James Nash
146. Paddy Floyd
147. Jimmy Armstrong
148. P. Murphy
149. Tom Daly
150. Paddy Minogue
151. Frank O'Brien
152. Dan Casey
153. P. Murphy
154. P. J. O'Halloran
155. Meda Ryan, *Biddy Early: The Wise Woman of Clare*, p. 81
156. T. Pyne, Ruan.
157. Meda Ryan, *Biddy Early: The Wise Woman of Clare*, pp. 87, 107
158. Liam Loughnane
159. Frank O'Brien
160. Jimmy Armstrong
161. P. Minogue
162. Thomas Hannon
163. Johnny Broderick
164. P. J. O'Halloran
165. Jim Daffy
166. P. J. O'Halloran

LONG AGO BY SHANNON SIDE
Edmund Lenihan

Long Ago by Shannonside is a heart-warming collection of colourful folktales and stories which were told around the turf fire in days gone by. There are stories about buried treasure, haunted places and strange meetings with the 'Good People'. We read about reactionary landlords, idio-syncratic priests and meet a host of local characters. Above all we see the people of Ireland at work and at play, in sorrow and in joy.

As every generation dies out part of their way of life dies with them. Already there is a whole generation of adults who have never enjoyed sitting by an open hearth in a that-ched cottage listening to the old people remembering the way they used to live.

Jimmy Armstrong, whose tales these are, possesses the gift of storytelling usually associated with the seanchaithe of long ago and his stories are guaranteed to entertain the reader.

STORIES OF OLD IRELAND FOR CHILDREN
Edmund Lenihan

Long ago in Ireland there were men who used to travel to the four ends of the earth and few travelled farther than Fionn and the men of the Fianna during their many exciting adventures. In *Stories of Old Ireland for Children* we read about 'Fionn Mac Cumhail and the Feathers from China', 'King Cormac's Fighting Academy' and 'Fionn and the Mermaids'.

Edmund Lenihan, one of Ireland's most popular storytellers, has collected these spell-binding tales which will delight and entertain children of all ages.